OMNISCRIPT

JONATHAN WADE BARROW

PAGE PUBLISHING
Conneaut Lake, PA

First originally published by Page Publishing 2023

Cover Artwork by Noa Hardisty

ISBN 979-8-88960-797-7 (pbk)
ISBN 979-8-88960-825-7 (digital)

Printed in the United States of America

CONTENTS

CHAPTER 1

THE AWAKENING

Pure, unbridled, infinite freedom—that was all Avior had ever known. The footprints behind him went on for miles, and as his toes pushed into the beautiful sand of the beach by the sea, he smiled to the sky. Each day he rose out of bed and enjoyed an absolutely sublime time in all he did.

It was bittersweet, though. He was born with a unique condition where his DNA caused the particles that made him up to align in such a way that he had been in danger. The doctors had made the call to upload his consciousness as an infant, a privilege usually exclusively reserved for elders before they physically passed away. He had lived peacefully here in the Simulation ever since.

But now all that was going to change. The doctors had notified him that they could now stabilize his particle alignment and he was going to be brought back to his physical body that lay waiting, now eighteen years of age.

Avior was excited to live a physical life, but he would miss the Simulation. The Simulation was infinite information, infinite accessible space, infinite possibilities, infinite perfection, and infinite beauty.

Avior knew that outside the Simulation, life had limitations, the physical laws of reality. Smiling again and with a wink at the sky, Avior instantaneously changed the appearance of his avatar. While he always kept his true visage that had been rendered in, he switched from a shaved head to long flowing blond hair. An exquisite silken white button-up popped onto his bare chest, and white jeans replaced his swim trunks. His childlike blue eyes had forever remained unchanged. With a final look at the ocean before him, he teleported off.

On the eve of his return to physical reality, Avior indulged himself one last time in all his favorite spaces in the Simulation. He first visited the Mars Colony and raced a rover between outposts. He even paused his rover race, entered a secret cheat code he had written, and glitched safely outside his space suit so he could stare at the Martian landscape unobstructed by his suit's visor.

After soaking up the sun for a moment, he accessed his menu and loaded Earth's Moon Base. He input his self-written cheat code again and bounded across the lunar terrain free of a space suit. After executing some low-gravity parkour moves, Avior stepped into the Moon Base and nabbed a snack in the food court. He smiled as others milled around the artfully architected atrium. Even though all the other avatars were young and fit, they were all cerebrally the elders from physical reality that had been uploaded, now able to spend an indefinite amount of time in the digital paradise of the Simulation.

It was getting late, and Avior wanted to say *goodbye* to those that mattered most to him. He had generations of relatives that lived here in the Simulation. During the early years of his life in the Simulation, his parents had chosen to be uploaded a little early so they could watch him develop. His family, here inside the Simulation, lived in a palatial forum called the *House of Aviideus*. It was a sprawling complex, blending interior and exterior spaces together where all his family lived.

With a pop, he teleported from the Moon Base to the open agora of the House of Aviideus. "Avior!" thundered about a hundred souls that were peacefully positioned throughout the amphitheaterlike space. Avior smiled and raised his right hand in greeting.

"So glad they got you fixed up back in the real world!" bellowed his great-uncle as he clapped a hand to Avior's shoulder.

"You go live a full, adventurous life out there, dear," breathed his great-grandmother excitedly. "Just know that we'll be here whenever you return."

Avior smiled like the simulated sun.

Even though most of the people living in the House of Aviideus were hundreds of years old, they were there before him, healthy and fit, beautiful and strong, and young and vibrant, with wisdom of great depth.

"Honey, oh, honey," his mother came over, followed by his father. "We are so proud of the powerful boy you have become. Go with vigor and live an extraordinary life. And make sure you find a supernova of a girl out there!"

Avior chuckled and winked at his dad.

"Go forth, son. There are great things to be done." Avior's father embraced him solidly, then released him.

Avior stood back and memorized his parents' faces one last time. His mother's dark curly hair. His father's tan chiseled features. Their posture, which conveyed great physical prowess. The starry sparkle in their eyes and the warmth of their smiling gaze. Avior punched a closed fist into an open hand of prayer, nodded, and then said, "I'll see you when I see you."

Avior turned and headed to his chambers. He needed to be asleep for the cerebral transfer from the Simulation to the physical world. That night his mind went on a flight illuminated by the simulated shine of a trillion stars' light.

"Avior? Avior, can you hear me?"

Avior laboriously opened his eyes. A team of doctors stood in a semicircle around him. "Avior, take it slowly. Your body has been continuously stimulated all these years. No need to worry about building back muscle. Your mind is used to controlling your avatar, so you should get the hang of your body in no time."

Avior grunted, then slowly sat up. Surprised at the ease, he looked down to see a tight, defined six-pack abdomen. "No kidding! Wow, you guys took really good care of me!"

The doctors nodded warmly, looking pleased. "We know how active you are in the Simulation, and while there may be a short span where you feel goofy, your brain has already developed an elevated level of coordination that we feel…"

Avior interrupted the doctor by doing a kick up off the bed and landing expertly in front of him.

"Ooh-kay, and the body introduction looks good," chuckled the doctor with a happy smile. "But now for the real news," he added seriously. "After studying you for nearly eighteen years, we made a startling discovery." The doctor glanced at the others and then back at Avior with a mixture of monumental solemnity and eagerness. "The alignment of your body's particles that made it necessary for us to upload your consciousness to the Simulation…Avior, your body was partially existing in another universe that we found to be intersecting our own."

Avior stared awestruck at the doctor, his mind racing. "How do you know? Do you have proof?" Avior asked.

The doctor looked straight at Avior. "Your body actually generated a single nucleotide. A single building block for DNA, the genetic code for all life. Except it's not from this life. Your body was partially existing in the fabric of reality of a different universe." The doctor was still looking straight at Avior. "We always figured if there was another universe, even infinitely more, that they would be outside our own. But you have found one, an intersecting universe, the Interverse if you will."

"What does this even mean?" Avior asked, still grappling with this information."

"Well," the doctor said with an intelligent twinkle in his eye, "after conducting tests, we found your one single nucleotide responded in a piezoelectric manner to physical pressure. Extrapolating that, we think that massive exertion of physical force will cause the Interverse's piezoelectric matter to generate energy. Extrapolating further, this stimulates biological processes. And extrapolating one last time, we believe it may be possible for you to generate a complete strand of this Interverse's DNA. However, we must hurry. Since we were able to stabilize your particle alignment, you'll only be able to phase into the Interverse one more time. One more time, and it needs to be in the near future." The doctor paused, letting this sink in. "There's a chance that some life-altering advances are in that DNA, Avior. The more physical force put in, the more powerful the piezoelectric energy is, which in turn creates the processes that generate that DNA that we could benefit from so greatly. We believe that if you sustain a level of physical exertion powerful enough and long enough, your body can craft a strand of Interverse DNA so potent, so pure, that we may be able to use it to cure the world of diseases, advance human evolution, halt aging, and so much more..." The doctor stared straight at Avior with hope glowing on his face. "It's the ultimate jewel of the universe. Two universes to be exact. We've even given a fitting name to this hypothetical DNA sequence: Omniscript."

A day passed, and all the while, Avior's head was spinning. Suddenly he had become the crux of the whole universe! "Unreal, this is unreal…" Avior quietly said aloud as he sat at a scenic spot called *China Walls* in his hometown of Honolulu, Hawaii. China Walls was a fifteen-foot-tall rock shelf that stood by the ocean. Here he had been called to meet the coach that would train him. With the ocean before him, he held his hands up in front of his face, looking at them with brand-new eyes in a whole new light. They looked alien to him.

Putting his hands down, he looked expectantly over his shoulder. He had been assigned a coach and a personal trainer to help guide him. From here on out, he would be undergoing nonstop physical trials to prepare himself for when he would force himself to align his particles, phase into Interverse space, and unleash his inner beast in the hope that the energy would stimulate the growth of the Omniscript in him.

"Hey!" a voice called out. Avior stood up quickly and turned. A tall tan chiseled man with long brown hair was coming toward him. Bouncing by his side was a thin athletic blonde girl that looked about his age. Avior winked involuntarily at her. She winked back without missing a beat.

"You must be Avior," the tall tan man said. "I'm Kai." He looked at Avior very seriously, but his eyes were gently smiling. "I'll be your coach. I've been briefed on your special…position." He looked Avior up and down straight as a laser. "Pretty crazy, yeah?" he said, letting a smile shine out.

"It's something else, all right," Avior said, acknowledging the situation.

A hand wave brought Avior's attention over to Kai's side. Holding her hand up, the blonde girl said, "Zovi Zelleven, personal trainer, pleased to meet you." As their eyes locked, Avior felt butterflies in his stomach, and a giddy cheer of happiness washed over him. His eyes flickered over her pixielike face and the glisten of her lips. Smiles.

Avior glanced skyward and cleared his throat professionally. "Well, let's get started, shall we?"

"Absolutely," Kai said. "I was told that your body was kept stimulated during your time in the Simulation. That's a relief. Your muscles should be honed and toned. What you are lacking off the bat is coordination, situational awareness, intuitive movement, and lightning-fast reaction time. Just to name a few."

"Geez, is that all?" Avior said, realizing he had more to work on than he had realized.

Kai smiled. "It will be challenging. But I have decades of experience to guide you with, and Zovi here"—Kai looked over at Zovi, as did Avior—"is going to complete these trials with you."

Avior was shocked for a moment; then relief breathed through him. "You're going to do all these challenges with me?" he asked her.

"I will do my best," Zovi said, looking at Avior very seriously. "But there will be times when you must go on alone. You will have to push yourself to levels that few can attain."

Kai nodded. "I chose this location to start with for two reasons. One, you will learn how to handle yourself accordingly while airborne. And two, it will be a fun introductory course to your challenges." Kai smiled.

Avior turned to look at the fifteen-foot-tall rock shelf that faced the ocean. "Oh, so we're just jumping?"

Kai and Zovi smiled at each other then smiled at Avior. "Hmm, it's so much more than just jumping," Zovi said. "With courage, you can really fly."

Despite his body being kept in shape, Avior was still adjusting to it. His first few jumps were basic: run, jump, soar toward the ocean, and then plunge into the warm water. Zovi, on the other hand, moved like a fluid through her jumps as she soared alongside Avior. Her sense of balance and serenity in the air was a real pleasure to witness. After a handful or two of just jumping, Kai called to Avior and Zovi from atop the wall, "Nice, nice, nice. I think you've got the basic jump. Let's move on to dives. Zovi, show Avior how it's done."

Zovi swam past Avior and flashed a toothy grin. "It's all about full commitment," she said pointedly.

"Run, jump, and fly superhero style straight at the water. I always put my hands out in front of me. It helps me balance during the flight."

Avior nodded, following her out of the water. He noticed that she was incredibly well-defined in her baby blue bikini.

Zovi executed a flawless swan-style dive as a demonstration for Avior. Having only done dives in the Simulation, Avior was confident in his ability to rough out a clean first attempt. "You got it!" Zovi called from the water below.

Avior leaned back, then darted forward and bounded out. "Oh shoot!" Avior yelped as he over-rotated and landed at a funny angle. Surfacing a moment later, he spit out salt water and looked over at Zovi.

She was laughing so hard a tear of joy was mixing into the beads of ocean on her face. "Oh, Avior, that was priceless! The 'Oh shoot' midway was golden!" Avior smiled a little, massaging his back that was stinging from the slap.

"It's all good, Avior!" Kai called down. "We're here to learn! Climb back up and give it another go!"

In no time, Avior was flying gracefully through the air with perfect swan dives. With Zovi and Kai talking him through his movements and demonstrating different techniques, Avior was able to quickly grasp the task at hand.

"Good, good, good," Kai stated solidly. "Zovi, let's move him on to flips."

Zovi nodded. Avior sized up China Walls again with a more discerning eye. "Okay now," Zovi said, "with front flips, you want to bound forward like you're going for a dive but you want to *tuck* your body into a ball just for a second and let it rotate. Got it?"

Avior thought it through for a moment. Again he had done flips in the Simulation, but as proven by his first dive, real-world physics was present here and not some glossy video game–style movements.

"Got it," Avior said. He stood still, body ready, thinking the movement through, eyes fixed on the edge of the rock wall.

"Go!" Kai shouted.

Avior sprang forward, mixing his knowledge from the Simulation with his new grasp of real-world physics. His feet hit the edge of the rock wall and popped his body up and out over the water. He snapped his arms tight around his legs for a split second, allowing that movement to rotate him head over heels. In that split second, he completed the flip as he flew through his airborne trajectory. In a moment of instinctive comprehension, he opened up out of his tuck and extended his body to its full length, effectively halting his rotation. It all worked perfectly, and he heard Kai and Zovi's cheers as he entered smoothly into the ocean, upright and facing the horizon.

"Thattaboy!" Kai hollered down.

"That's what I'm talking about!" Zovi yelled.

The training progressed as the sun soared overhead. To accompany his jumps, dives, and front flips, Kai and Zovi coached him through backflips, gainers, vortex dives, front flip 360s, front flip to dive, and double front flips. He slapped a couple of belly flops and back-splats along the way, but his split-second decision-making abilities skyrocketed as he persevered and successfully landed each movement.

The sun was nearing the horizon by the time Kai put his fingers in his mouth and blew a shrill whistle to Zovi and Avior, who were talking the tricks through in the ocean below. "That's it, guys! Let's wrap it up for the day. Come on up here!" Kai called.

Exhausted, dripping wet, and head spinning from all the flips, Avior stood with Zovi in front of Kai a moment later. "That was a great first day," Kai said proudly. "A nice introduction to the challenges ahead. I wanted to start our journey off with a bit of fun," Kai winced, then continued, "Not all the challenges we will do will be rainbows and butterflies. Some will be arduous, yes, but they will be rewarding. They are necessary too." Kai directed his attention solely to Avior. "In order to really generate the force needed to encourage your Interverse DNA to bloom, we're going to have to go full savage on some challenges."

Avior took that as a bit of a blow. *If learning complicated airborne maneuvers and taking full body splats repeatedly on the ocean were the easy part, he was in for a rough ride ahead*, he thought to himself. He grimaced slightly as he returned Kai's strong stare. "I am ready to move forward. I know the immense prize of what can be gained through this."

All three of them stood silently for a moment. "Good, we will move forward. I will contact you shortly with our next training challenge."

With that, Kai shook Avior's hand, set his sight on the setting sun, and then turned and departed. From over his shoulder, Kai said, "Zovi, see Avior off."

Avior and Zovi were both exhausted, and in a shared stare, they let out laughs. "Nice work today," Zovi said, lightly punching Avior's arm.

"Thanks. I'm so used to being in the Simulation that the real world feels like one that is simulated. Except for the pain." Avior massaged his upper back. "Boy, I've never felt pain before. Those belly flops and back-splats hurt like something else."

Zovi grinned tomboyishly. "Ah, you'll toughen up. Don't you worry. Bumps and bruises build character." She chuckled and let her eyes take in Avior's face. Avior blushed a little but also let his eyes move across Zovi's pixielike face. They both chuckled, then dropped their gazes to the ground for a moment. "Cool. Nice moves, Mr. Digital Boy," Zovi said with a wink, looking at Avior's face again. Avior couldn't help but smile from ear to ear. "See you for the next one," Zovi said, bumping Avior's knuckles. With a little flick of her long blonde hair, Zovi spun on the spot and headed off at a trot.

Avior watched her go, feeling lighthearted and invigorated. *What a whirlwind,* he thought. He had just blasted out of a simulated dream and grabbed hold of mankind's destiny, and now he had a blonde pixie-faced babe glimmering in his eye.

CHAPTER 2

RUN IT

Kai gave Avior a day of contemplation the next day. The coach wanted Avior to absorb his training at China Walls, do light stretching, and take time to recuperate. *Easy enough*, Avior thought. Avior completed this light duty gratefully from the comfort of his small condominium that the government had provided him as a gesture for what he had agreed to do in return.

It was a modest place. Situated on the tenth floor on the edge of Waikiki, he had a floor-to-ceiling corner view of the ocean and the sky-rises that lined the district. Since he was in his body safely for the first time in his life, and he had a day to himself, he took time to give himself good grooming.

He ran a brush over his thick light-brown hair, first parting it on one side, then the other. He stared at his reflection in the mirror for a long time. Oddly enough, his virtual face that had matured inside the Simulation was remarkably close to how his natural face had grown to look here in the real world. He moved his face from side to side, admiring his strong jaw and high cheekbones. He had a very straight brow, with thick eyebrows, and sapphire-blue hunter eyes that remained ever watchful like a happy hawk. He smiled. His nose had a boyish Peter Pan look to it. All his features, partnered together with the straightforward teen exuberance that shone through him, gave him a poster boy image, he supposed. He glanced out the floor-to-ceiling window at the ocean. *He was a poster boy, to be honest*, he thought to himself.

What kind of poster boy, he wasn't sure. His future seemed heavy on his shoulders as he thought about it. If he could complete all the challenges that lay ahead and generate the energy and force needed, and if everything worked and the doctors and scientists could extract the Interverse DNA…he would be the face of advancing humankind.

Avior ran his fingers through his hair and looked at the bright blue sky out the window. *That's a lot of pressure on one person*, he thought. Thankfully, his phone rang, breaking the heavy cloud of thoughts that hung over him. "Hello?" Avior asked.

"Avior, its Zovi. Listen, I know you're probably lost in thought. I am too, but tomorrow we're hitting it hard. Hopefully putting ourselves into action and progressing along this path will clear our minds. Kai asked me to tell you that we are going to start a running segment. That's all he told me. I don't know if he wants sprinting, long distance, or what."

Avior was relieved. Running. Simple, straight-forward, paced, running. "Oh, okay, that sounds all right. I'm still a little concerned about the challenges ahead, but this one I feel super confident I can tackle," Avior said, making sure to convey his confidence with strength.

"Great! Meet Kai and me at the University of Hawaii track tomorrow at dawn." Zovi hung up at that.

Avior held the phone for a moment. Part of him had wanted to talk to Zovi for a while, but maybe it was good that they stay professional. Avior sighed. The first real girl he had met and he already had a bit of a crush. With a roguish smile, he kicked back and watched a little TV as the sky slowly morphed into twilight out his window.

The next morning, at dawn, Avior walked purposefully out onto the University of Hawaii track. He was dressed for action. Running shoes, running shorts, a muscle shirt, and a couple of bottles of water in his backpack. As he stepped onto the outer lane of the track, he spotted Kai and Zovi conversing down the straightaway at the starting line.

As he neared, Kai bellowed out, "Morning there, trooper!" Zovi smiled radiantly by his side. "We're going to get right to it. I want to see your best mile time. Zovi got here early and knocked out a 6:12. Pretty quick, yeah?" Kai pressed. "You think you can beat that?"

Avior raised his eyebrows and nodded at Zovi. He had never run a mile before, much less a timed one. He didn't even know if that was supreme time or a more easy-paced one. Not letting his thoughts show on his face, Avior put his backpack off to the side then stood tall at the starting line. He ran his eyes around the track, trying to gauge what kind of time he could do. "Um, how many laps is it?" Avior asked, unsure.

"Oh! Right you are! I've got to remind myself how fresh to the world you are. Four laps, you ready?" Kai asked encouragingly.

Four laps, no problem, Avior thought. He better give it 110 percent though; it wouldn't look good if he got a mediocre time since all this was for him. "Ready," Avior said stoically.

"Right! Okay, ready, on your mark, get set, GO!" Kai shouted, blowing a whistle.

Avior was off like a rocket. *Oh, this felt good,* Avior thought to himself. He forgot about his clouded thoughts, and the purity of the movement brought clarity to his mind. *Pacing was not going to be a good example*, he thought. He broke into a full sprint. He forced himself, despite his discomfort, to hold a full sprint. Lap one, boom, done. Lap two, boom, done. Lap three, boom, done. He was tearing up the track on his last lap, panting hard, but in a rhythm. He forced himself with all his strength to maintain that full sprint and, muscles rippling, crossed the finish line to the applause of Zovi.

"Wow! That was just a pure unfettered sprint the whole way!" Zovi exclaimed.

Avior was exhausted but felt elated. "Time?" He asked, looking over at Kai.

"Five thirteen, I'll be darned, that was an incredible first mile for you, big congratulations," Kai said proudly.

"Holy frick!" Avior heaved, trying to catch his breath. "So that was that! Okay, okay, got it!" Avior said, thankful he had done so well.

"Zovi, pace Avior for a two-lap cooldown jog, please and thank you," Kai commanded with his authoritative voice.

Zovi grabbed Avior by the elbow, and they both jogged off at an easy pace around the track. "Pure running is just the warm-up," Zovi said to Avior by her side.

"The warm-up to what?" Avior asked curiously, still catching his breath.

"Kai wants to push you into parkour. You know, free running with flips between obstacles," Zovi said, glancing sideways at Avior.

Avior blasted out a laugh. "Oh goodness! Now that is the best news I've heard all day! I love parkour! I used to glitch around the Simulation popping fat flips all over the Mars Colony, the Moon Base, and a million exotic locations all over. Sheesh, parkour is my bread-and-butter baby!" Avior exclaimed happily.

Zovi's face blossomed into a Cheshire Cat smile. "Oh! Wow! Well shoots then, that means today is going to be awesome! I was worried it would be hard for you to learn the techniques for today's challenges."

Avior shot Zovi a savvy smile. They competed the cooldown laps, then met back up with Kai at the starting line.

"All right, so we are going to progress to free running with heavy elements of parkour. The University of Hawaii campus is a perfect place to train. I studied the playback footage of you in the Simulation," Kai said, looking impressed as he gazed at Avior. "It seems you already have a nice knack for the sport."

Avior stood sure-footed and squared up with confidence to Kai. "Yes, indeed, I am a competent athlete in that field." He winked at Zovi. She smiled back.

"Good. No need to take baby steps. We will go full steam ahead," Kai said smartly.

They left the track and made their way into the heart of the campus. There was a plethora of obstacles and architecture surrounding them here, providing an ample area to train in. "Okay, now I've seen the footage of you, Avior, and I want to see that same power and prowess here," Kai said. "Zovi, stay with me. Let's give Avior our full attention."

Avior sized up the surrounding space, noting every ledge, gap, wall, nook, and cranny. Just as Avior was about to start, a lone figure descended from a third-story roof by a light pole then sprinted forward, throwing a quick front flip on flat ground, then konged over a wall, flew across a grassy gap, and landed a precision on a planter ledge.

Avior glanced at Kai. Kai was looking over at the boy with a sparkle in his eye. "You there! Come over here!" Kai shouted across the way. The boy hopped off the planter ledge and then jogged over to the trio. "What's your name, son?" Kai asked the boy.

"Midas, Midas Modiavelli."

Kai looked from Midas to Avior with a gleam in his eye. "Perfect. My name's Kai. This here is Zovi." Midas smiled handsomely at Zovi. "Midas, would you be interested in a friendly competition with my athlete here?" Midas looked over at Avior. "This is Avior Aviideus," Kai told Midas. "We are doing extensive training, and for both of your benefits, I propose a parkour match. The athlete with the most tricks in a line, level of technical difficulty, and best style wins. Whattaya say? Interested?"

Midas smirked smugly, "Sure, I could use a bit of fun." He squinted keenly at Avior then said, "I'll go first." He darted off with an expert-level adroitness in his movement. *Midas was an extremely skilled athlete, no question about that*, Avior thought. Avior remained unfazed, though, as he watched Midas vortex dive roll over a wall, front flip between two concrete pillars, kong gainer off a first-story balcony, and barrel roll from atop a sculpture. Exhausted and panting, Midas halted and made an "X" gesture with his arms raised.

"Excellent. Avior?" Kai said aside to Avior.

As impressive as Midas's tricks were, Avior held steadfast in his grasp of his own abilities. All his parkour knowledge was virtual, but it was wired in his brain, and his training at China Walls had unlocked body control for him here in the real world. Kai raised a hand and bellowed, "Go!"

Avior took off and did back-to-back ticktack side flips off alternating legs on two trees that were close together. He heard Zovi cheer from behind him, and he smiled. His confidence bolstered; he climbed the eave of a building and charged the edge of the moderately high roof. With a tight spring-out off the roof, he tucked into a ball and rotated a perfect double front flip, landing with a commando-style rollout to soften the impact. He caught a glimpse of Midas for a fraction of a second; he had his hands on his hips, and his brow furrowed. Avior lowered his head and bull-charged forward. He leaped up a flight of stairs, quickly tossing a smooth front flip at the top, then shot toward a gap between two brick walls. With all the force he could muster, he launched out, hucking a muscly gainer full over the gap. Landing deftly, he dropped off the brick wall, side-flipped on the spot, and then immediately palm-flipped off the brick wall. Landing solid, he held still for a moment.

"Well, I'll be a monkey's uncle!" He heard Kai laugh out loud as he clapped his big hands.

"Yeah, Avior! That's how you do it right there!" Zovi squealed. Midas looked off into the distance. He knew Avior's run had trumped his own.

"All right, boys, bring it in, bring it in," Kai called stoutly from across the way. Avior and Midas jogged over across the grass. "Midas, thank you for the competition there," Kai said warmly. "Avior, I'm glad your introduction to your body was so quick. I was worried we'd have trouble getting you started. Seems your grasp of physics has translated well."

"Introduction to your body?" Midas questioned, looking confusedly at Kai and then at Avior.

Avior glanced at Kai, silently communicating he'd take this one. "I grew up in the Simulation. I just recently got reintroduced to my body after quite a long time."

"No way!" Midas exclaimed. "No wonder your style is so butter, and those tricks…I was figuring you must have trained relentlessly in a foam pit in a gym…" Midas sized up Avior with a new comprehension in his eyes. "Yo, you're going to go far. Throwing those kinds of moves this early on…" Midas grinned. "Avior Aviideus, I'll remember that, you're a core player, that's for sure."

"You know, now that I think about it," Kai interrupted, "how would you like to train with us? I have a strict regimen of challenges set up for Avior, and Zovi here"—Kai gestured to Zovi, who was by his side—"is Avior's personal trainer. She guides Avior and chips in when needed for pacing purposes, but it would be beneficial to our goals if you'd be willing to compete with Avior."

"Ho! A strict regimen, you say? I could use that. What's the goal? Some kind of triathlon?" Avior, Zovi, and Kai exchanged concerned looks. Revealing the fact that there was a newly discovered universe and that Avior was the vessel for prospective alien DNA that could catapult humankind forward into a new age was a bit much to tell a kid they had just met.

"His training is leading toward a sort of grand exhibition of power and prowess," Kai said, solidifying the goal and yet keeping it secret. Avior and Zovi nodded at Midas. Telling someone you must align your particles to immerse into an intersecting universe and exert the energy of a berserking barbarian at war just wouldn't sound real at all.

Midas smiled. "Oh, right on! A grand exhibition! That sounds about where I'd like my training to take me too. Yep, count me in. I'd love to take on these challenges you've planned."

"It's settled then. Midas, welcome to the team!" Kai exclaimed. "All right now, let's jog a lap around campus. Avior, Midas, and Zovi, you three take the lead. I'll bring up the rear and keep an eye on things. I want to see parkour movements on every obstacle we come across. This lap is going to burn a little. I can guarantee that." Kai pointed forward and began jogging. *Kai was surprisingly springy in his step*, Avior thought, as he leaned forward and started jogging.

Their lap around campus was indeed a burning exercise. Every gap, stair set, wall, and low rooftop they came across, Avior, along with Midas and Zovi, sprang into action, rotating flip after flip. They each had a sketchy landing or two along the way; Midas even tripped off a high ledge and fell flat on his back into a thick bush. They all helped him out of the tangle and got a good laugh out of it. As they came back around to where they had started, they all had sore abdomens, calves, and quads from the burning workout.

"Nicely done, nicely done. That's a wrap on today's training. Avior, Zovi, and Midas, we will be in the ocean tomorrow. Swimsuits on for training, got it? Sandy Beach at dawn. We are going to hit it hard, but it should be fun," Kai said warmly but with an edge in his voice as he tossed a shaka with his right hand. "Okay, I've got a few things I need to take care of. You all have a good evening. I'll see you at sunrise." With that, Kai departed, leaving the trio feeling accomplished after their successful day of training.

"I wonder what Kai wants us to train for at Sandy's," Midas said.

"I've seen the itinerary, but Kai told me to follow his lead and let him coach how he sees fit. I can't say anything other than it should be a blast!" Zovi said with ocean eyes.

"I've never been to Sandy's Beach. What's it like?" Avior asked curiously.

Zovi and Midas exchanged a knowing look. "It's a super wavy beach," Zovi said excitedly. "Big waves and a big stretch of shore. It's one of the most dynamic beaches on the island."

Midas nodded. "Yeah, man, you'll love it," he said to Avior. "I gotta say, I've never had a proper coach before. I'm looking forward to having someone push me. I usually train within my comfort zone. It's going to be nice having someone force me outside that realm into higher levels."

Zovi nodded in agreement. "Yes, and there's no one better to lead us through these challenges than Kai. He's medaled in competition in every single one of the sports he is training us in."

Avior and Midas started in surprise. "Oh! There it is. I didn't know what sport he was professional at," Avior said awestruck. "Dang, it's nice to know he's pro at ALL of them." He exchanged an impressed grin with Midas.

The trio talked for a while, relaxing their muscles and stretching as they did so. After a while, Midas chimed in, "Okay, guys, I'm heading out. My mom is making dinner, and I'm kinda beat."

Avior and Zovi shook Midas's hand and gave him a pat on the shoulder. "We'll see you tomorrow bright and early," Zovi said gently. "Get some rest. You're going to need it." She winked with a smile.

Midas nodded appreciatively, then jogged off across the grass, heading home. "Well, good day today," Avior said to Zovi. He was happy but a little nervous to be alone with Zovi, especially with daylight changing into the romantic colors of sunset and twilight.

"Yup, you did great, Avior," she said with a bit of a quieter hush in her voice now than how she had spoken when Midas had been present. Avior's heart did a flip that could have competed with his parkour earlier. "I think you're off to a brilliant start," she said, still with that hint of that hush in her voice. "You've got quite a tough journey ahead, not going to lie. I've seen what Kai has planned for you to equip you for the sheer ferocity of force they say you'll have to exert when the time comes."

Avior adjusted his shoulders, thinking of what lay ahead. He was still processing what his future held, and he still wasn't even sure what it was. But he knew he was going to have to buck up and be ready to face a future that nobody had ever had. Ever.

Zovi was reading his face as his thoughts poured forth. A small twitch of worry flickered over her forehead, then disappeared. She smiled reassuringly. "Avior, we'll be here for you, all the way through everything." She was looking at him, all her focus looking him straight in his right eye. "All this could have happened to someone else. But it happened to you. Just accept that you are 'the chosen one.' That it is you, and nobody else." She leaned in and gave him a warm hug. She held him for a long moment, then stepped back. "See you tomorrow, 'Mr. Chosen One.'" She winked and giggled then waved and walked off into the beautiful colors of the twilight that had descended upon them.

CHAPTER 3

FLUID MOVEMENTS

After a night of much-needed rest, Avior was out the door the next morning before the sun had risen. Kai was waiting in his pickup truck in the parking lot of Avior's condo with Zovi riding shotgun and Midas stretched out in the back of the truck's bed with the surfboards.

"Hurry up, slowpoke!" Midas jokingly taunted.

"Morning, Avior," Zovi said with a smile from the window of the passenger side.

"Rise and shine there, champ!" Kai called as he put the truck into drive.

Avior waved and climbed into the back of the truck with Midas. Kai revved and pulled the truck out from around the condo onto Kalakaua Avenue, then cruised off up the road.

"I'm pretty excited. Today should be a really solid training bout," Midas commented evenly as he peered out at the horizon atop the ocean.

Avior breathed deeply as the wind whipped his hair around. "Ditto. I practically sprang out of bed this morning," Avior said, looking at Midas across from him, then turning his head and squinting at the horizon as well.

He heard a pleasant melody in the air from the radio and looked over at Kai and Zovi seated in the cab. His heart flipped a little as he noticed Zovi was wearing a soft pink bikini. He smiled and drifted off into daydreams as the beauty of everything whirled around him on the way to Sandy Beach.

"The water looks great today!" Kai called over his shoulder to the boys as the truck came around a bend and the beach came into view. A moment later, they were parked and clambering out of the truck to stand and scope out the scene. "Yup! It's good today," Kai commented as he stared out over the beach at the waves breaking just offshore.

Zovi turned to face Avior and Midas, "You guys ready?"

Midas punched Avior's arm. "You betcha. Bro, let's get it. Coach, what's the game plan?" Midas asked Kai.

"Glad you asked!" Kai said enthusiastically. "You three are going to go out and start on the left side of the beach and swim ALL the way across to the far right, then come ALL the way back. That's the warm-up. I've got a good training session worked out for you guys today." Kai smiled and pointed to the ocean. "Now get to it! First one to finish wins a free lunch from the taco truck!" The three teens laughed, looking at each other, then jumped to it and took off across the beach at a run.

Avior felt elated as he dove into the inviting ocean. As he swam out through the baby blue waves, he glanced to his left and saw Midas. Glancing to his right, he saw Zovi, looking incredible in her soft pink bikini. He pushed everything aside, at least for the moment. He needed this win. He needed to prove to Kai that he was fulfilling his duty.

He passed where the waves were breaking, then immediately turned right and started swimming across the expansive stretch of ocean. Avior opted for the freestyle method of swimming out of a natural ease of body movement. As he took a breath, he noticed Midas had chosen the breaststroke. On his next breath, he saw Zovi executing a beautiful butterfly stroke. They were all neck and neck, slipstreaming through the water super smoothly. A rogue wave that was cresting farther out than the others forced the three teens to dive down to avoid being pulled over the falls. Avior looked up from beneath to see the wave tube up into a barrel, forming a gorgeous sapphire cylinder above him. The team of three charged on, feeling vigorous and happy. They all hit the far end of the beach at about the same time and looped back around, swimming with all their energy across the stretch toward the finish line.

As Avior swam on as fast as he could, he checked quickly to his left and right on Midas and Zovi. In his peripheral vision, he saw a fin off to his side. Alarmed, he glanced over. Sure enough, a fin was moving through the water, between them and the beach. "Shark!" Avior screamed. Midas and Zovi looked around in alarm. The fin was a little behind them, but it was nearer to the beach than they were and moving in their direction. "Keep going forward, keep going forward!" Avior yelled. The trio were now swimming for their lives. Muscles burning, with fear clouding his mind, Avior swam forward with all his might. If they could get ahead of the shark more, they'd be able to swim over toward the beach and make a safe getaway.

In what seemed like a second, Avior, Zovi, and Midas had passed the place where they had started their warm-up race. The fin was directly behind them now, by about twenty or thirty feet, which meant they had a clear shot to swim over to the beach. They swam like animals through the waves, and as soon as they had sand to stand on, they splashed forward up onto the beach as fast as they could. "Oh my god!" Midas yelled, exhausted, looking over at the fin behind them. Zovi collapsed on the beach, shaking to her core. Avior stared horror-struck at the fin, knowing they had just barely missed a grisly end.

"Well, I'll be…you all tied for the finish…guess I owe you three lunch. That's a dolphin by the way," Kai said gently, standing behind them on the beach. "Brah! You guys never seen a dolphin before or what?"

A Hawaiian girl exclaimed as she walked over carrying a surfboard. "I saw you guys out there panicking, but boy you sure were going ham on that li'l swim. You all racing or somethin'?" she asked, looking at all four of them.

"Training," Kai said coolly. "Are you getting ready to paddle out and surf?"

The girl grinned, "I sure am. Me and that dolphin, yeah?" She laughed gently. "Sorry to poke fun, but that was a whole situation right there. I'm Cove Cordova, nice to meet you all. But for real though, if you all are paddling out, I can show you the ropes. This break is called *Pipe Littles*."

"All right, Cove Cordova," Kai said graciously, "give my team here a second to collect themselves, and then they'll join you out there."

Cove nodded, then trotted across the beach with a plucky air, got in the water, and paddled out. "Well, guys, sorry you had a scare, but let's not let that put a damper on things. Hydrate, then grab your boards. Midas, are you a surfer?" Kai asked.

"Not really, but I'm a quick learner," Midas said.

"Good, good." Kai said. "Avior has virtual surfing abilities. He should be able to pick up the real thing quickly too. Zovi is a competent surfer, and our girl Cove out there is willing to lend a hand," Kai winked as he made a swirling motion with a raised finger. "Hydrate, then hit it. I wanna see you three getting barreled."

A moment later, Avior, Zovi, and Midas were back in the game as they paddled out to Pipe Littles.

Cove waved them over as they got out to the spot. "All right, guys, this one is big, fast, gets you pitted, and breaks in shallow water. Don't allow yourself to be in a situation where you're going to get pulled over the falls on a wave. Always get low if you're going down and duck dive these suckas. They're strong ones, yeah?" She chuckled. Avior caught Midas's eyes roving over Cove. Avior smiled and looked over at Zovi. She looked back, and they shared a smile.

Avior had been an extremely adept surfer in the Simulation, and if picking up the real thing was the same as their dive training at China Walls and their free running at the University of Hawaii, he felt confident he'd do just fine. Cove wasn't kidding around when it came time for action. She paddled fiercely into a large cresting wave and stood up in a split second, streaking forward for a moment before ducking down to tuck into a beautiful barrel. She shot out the end of the barrel and carved around on the face of the wave then popped up over the top of the lip and dropped down onto her board and paddled straight back out to the trio. "Yuh!" she called across the water.

Zovi smiled, then glanced around to see another sizable wave headed their way. She paddled eagerly in front of it, then dropped in on it and stood up, flicking back her wet blonde ponytail. Avior and Midas watched happily as Zovi dragged her hand on the face of the wave to slow herself and dig deeper into the barrel. "So pitted!" Midas chuckled as they heard Zovi let out an "Ohhh" from inside the barrel.

"Yeah, girl!" Cove called with approval. They heard clapping in the distance and looked over to see Kai looking on cheerfully.

"All right, I'm going for it!" Midas yelled over his shoulder at Avior as he started muscling for the next wave. Midas was, for sure, a beginner surfer, and it was apparent as he fought for the wave. He missed the wave, slapping the water with his hand in frustration.

"No worries, here comes a good one!" Avior shouted over to him. This time, Midas gave it everything he had as he paddled for the wave. He caught it, and with a wobbly pop, he got to his feet as he dropped down the face of it. No sooner had he shot down the face of the wave when his surfboard pearled under the wave and he flew head over heels into the water. Avior, Zovi, and Cove looked on with curiosity, then saw Midas get pulled up over the falls as the wave went over. His butt was visible atop the breaking wave for a moment before he was thrown over the falls. A moment later, he surfaced and belted out a laugh. "Ho! Well, there you have it! Mr. Head-Over-Heels here!" he shouted out. Avior, Zovi, and Cove smiled at him.

"You're next, Mr. Simulation," Zovi said across the water to Avior with a smirk. Avior nodded; he felt sure of himself. Still he stayed laser-focused, as he wanted to maintain 100 percent effort in each challenge that Kai prepared for him. He looked over his shoulder and saw a massive rouge wave charging toward him. "Get it! Get it! Get it!" Cove shouted, seeing it too.

Avior buckled down and paddled with all his might. The wave caught up to him, and all of Avior's training in the Simulation that was wired in his brain kicked in instantaneously. He popped up into a savage stance and dropped down the face of the wave, streaking straight forward. He immediately swerved back onto the face and slashed a spray high in the air. The wave began to barrel, and Avior ran his whole arm along the face, slowing him so he could get absolutely shacked in the massive wave. He fell back so deep into the barrel he could barely see from all the liquid mist flying around.

All thoughts of the Simulation fell away as the breathtaking beauty of this organic reality shone through the chandelier roof of the cerulean wave as it barreled relentlessly over his head. Perfection. *It doesn't get any better than this*, Avior thought. Except it did. He saw Zovi's pixielike face out through the barrel as she stared awestruck at his massive catch. That moment clicked in his mind like a snapshot. In those split-second moments, he knew that vision right there in the barrel would be imprinted in him for life.

With a great misty spit of pent-up force from inside the tube, Avior blasted out of the barrel, zooming across the smooth blue water. Kai roared his approval, raising his hands and cheering as Avior cruised proudly atop his surfboard. Zovi, Midas, and Cove erupted with a congratulatory celebration at

Avior's absolutely triumphant tube. "Ho! That one can shred, yeah?" Cove said loudly to Zovi. Zovi nodded, smiling, not taking her eyes off Avior.

The four teens sessioned Pipe Littles for hours. Midas eventually started catching waves, still a little shakily. Cove was a natural. She told the other three that she had been surfing as long as she could remember. She offered helpful pointers and tips to each of them as they surfed wave after wave in the sun's rays.

Avior was still giving it 100 percent, 100 percent of the time. He also found himself looking at Zovi quite a lot. It was hard not to; the soft pink bikini she had on was like eye candy to him. And to his astonishment, he found that she looked at him more than often as well, often holding his gaze for long moments. *She was probably just doing her job*, Avior thought, but her eyes were full and inquisitive and sometimes lingered longer than seemed professionally necessary for a personal trainer.

"Lunch! Bring it on in, you guys! Cove, come with us. I'll get you lunch too!" Kai called across the water to the four new friends. The four of them paddled in from the session and put their boards in the sand. They all met up at the taco truck parked in the lot, and Kai ordered them all garlic shrimp tacos. "You all are getting water to drink, though," Kai said sternly with a bit of a wink. "You need to hydrate. It's not good to drink soda after a workout." They all obliged and enjoyed their delicious garlic shrimp tacos with ice-cold water as they sat on the curb of the lot overlooking Sandy Beach.

"Great surfing out there, you guys," Kai commented between bites. "Avior, you absolutely killed it. I'm glad you took it upon yourself to become so skilled in the Simulation and that you're putting in the focus and effort so determinedly here with us in the real world." Avior bobbed his head, thankful to hear Kai's kind words. "Zovi, beautiful surfing out there. I had no doubt in my mind you'd be a key role model for the others to see," Kai continued. "Midas, good start. Little topsy-turvy at first, but you got a handle on it. Keep at it, and I'm sure you'll be able to incorporate your parkour skills into surfing. I know guys that throw all kinds of flip airs off the lip of the waves," he said. "And Cove, Little Miss Plucky. I said this to Midas just the other day to recruit him, but I could use competent, capable athletes to help Avior here train for an event he has coming up soon. Would you be interested in joining our little party here? We will be training almost nonstop from here on out. Avior's event is coming up soon. I could use a skilled girl like yourself on the team. Whattaya think?"

Cove's face had been lighting up as Kai spoke, "Oh! So you're a coach? I thought you were a dad!"

Avior, Zovi, and Midas laughed out loud. Kai chuckled to himself and looked at her. "Well? Do you want to join the team?"

Cove looked sideways at Avior, then over at Zovi and Midas. Midas was a bit googly-eyed; he was unashamed of showing his attraction to her. Cove saw him and giggled appreciatively, "Yeah, you guys look like a lot of fun. Plus, I've got surf contests I want to enter later this year, and this training will be super beneficial for me. I'm in." They all clapped in applause as a welcoming gesture, with Midas even patting Cove on the back.

Avior felt relieved. Adding teammates to train with was helping ease the pressure he felt burdening him. The comradery was building with each new addition to the team. He had felt overwhelmed a few days ago, but with the love and support of Kai and Zovi, and now with Midas and Cove to help spur him, he felt like he might be able to generate the Omniscript once he aligned into the Interverse.

Kai had the four friends swim one last lap across the beach and back as a cooldown. This time the dolphin from before was back, and it had brought its pod with it. Twenty dolphins swam alongside Avior and the others as they muscled their way through the water. Bodies taut from all the exercise of the day, the four friends felt extremely accomplished as they trooped up out of the water after their lap.

"Tomorrow is going to be a rough one," Kai said as they came up the beach. "Everyone is going to get pretty worked, so we're going to call it a day a little early so you all can rest this evening." He nodded authoritatively to each of them in turn, turning off his charm for a moment and flexing his position as coach. They all nodded in understanding.

Cove headed to her Jeep and waved *good night* to Avior and the others. Avior and Midas hopped into the back of Kai's truck, and a moment later, they turned out of Sandy Beach's parking lot and sped back toward town. A little while later, back at Avior's Waikiki condo, he happily bid everyone a good evening. A quick fist bump with Midas, a handshake with Kai, and a gentle hug with Zovi, who, he noticed, held him a little longer than he expected. Avior felt incredible after such a successful day of training. He rode the elevator up to the tenth floor, made his way into his condo, and washed up.

That night he watched the entirety of the sunset out the window, allowing his mind to replay every moment of the day. That one mental snapshot, where he was looking out of the barrel at Zovi's pixielike face, remained at the forefront of his mind until he drifted off into a deep slumber, with just a sliver of starlight shining promisingly through his window.

CHAPTER 4

FIGHTING STYLES

The next morning, Avior grabbed a banana off his countertop on the way out the door. Kai was waiting in his truck with Zovi and Midas, the usual hustle and bustle of Waikiki streaming around them in the early morning sun. Zovi waved enthusiastically, and Midas tossed a shaka up with his right hand. Kai looked serious this morning but still greeted Avior with a "Mornin' there, bucko."

Kai drove them all in his truck through Waikiki, which was an absolute dream that morning. There was Kapi'olani Park with its dewy grass and big banyan trees, the seaside aquarium, the beautiful zoo, and the jungle of sky-rises. Once they got right in the heart of Waikiki, Kai took a side street, and pulled up to a building with a sign that said, "Yolo Dojo."

Avior exchanged raised eyebrows with Midas, and Zovi turned around in her seat to give them a furrowed brow. "Today, we fight," Kai said, looking at the building. Avior took a second to let that sink in. He had figured they might cover martial arts, but that time was now here, and he knew Kai would expect the best out of him.

"Tight! I bet I can give someone a good clock across the jaw!" Midas said eagerly. Zovi giggled, then glanced at Avior. Avior summoned forth a surge of primal energy and nodded curtly at her, then hopped out of the truck and made his way toward Yolo Dojo, alone. Kai closed his truck door, a smile of approval on his lips as he watched Avior stride forward.

The inside of Yolo Dojo was expansive. There was a gym area with exercise equipment, a large mat floor area for combat sparring, and a mixed martial arts cage with bleachers surrounding it for an audience. "Ho! Morniiiiiing!" Cove said as she walked out of the girls' locker room dressed in animal-print form fitting clothes. Midas openly gawked for a moment before Avior elbowed him playfully in the ribs to snap him back. "Thanks for letting me know the spot, Kai. It looks like the back of that truck is getting full, and I love to drive my trusty Jeep anyway," she said.

Kai nodded, eyeing up the area. "I want to start you guys just warming up with the exercise machines and weights. I want you to push yourselves, not strain yourselves. Don't overdo it. You need to save strength for the combat training after the warm-up." He looked at Avior but spoke to them all. "Touch base with each machine. I want all your muscles warmed up feeling honed and toned." Avior and Midas headed over to the free weights, while Zovi and Cove made their way to the leg press machine and the chest fly machine. Kai walked over to the boxing ring and began speaking with an impressively built athlete, out of earshot.

Avior and Midas were decently built for eighteen and figured they'd pump a twenty-five-pound dumbbell in each hand, alternating between left and right with each pump. "Frick, this is going to get us ripped in no time," Midas commented after a couple of reps, massaging his bicep.

"No kidding," Avior said. "Put some time in with these, and you could give that clock on the jaw you were talking about pretty well."

Midas chuckled as he glanced over his shoulder at Cove. "Bro, you think I have a shot with Cove?" Midas asked. Avior's eyes widened innocently as he thought of his own attraction to Zovi.

"Just be her friend first. See if any sparks fly, yeah?"

Midas nodded, smiling.

Cove was incredibly attractive, Avior thought. She was very gregarious, unabashedly herself, and her athletic body was a deep smooth brown tone, which made her look like a Tahitian beauty under a waterfall.

"What do you think of Zovi?" Midas asked Avior. "You guys just professional, or you got a li'l twinkle in your eye for her?" he pressed slyly.

Avior was reluctant to divulge his feelings, but he was an open, honest person, and he decided to be straight with Midas. "Well, she's my personal trainer, you know? She gives me pointers and tips off to the side and advises me here and there on how to manage my body." Avior paused for a moment, then continued, "But I'll be honest, I like her. And I mean, she looks great. She's definitely a pleasure to look at. Plus, she's a bright, sunshiny, sparkly girl."

"Ooh, got a li'l crushy crush, do ya?" Midas smirked knowingly through cheekily squinted eyes.

Avior returned to pumping his dumbbells, but he had a tiny smile on the corner of his lips.

Across the way, Zovi and Cove were having a similar conversation. "I noticed Midas keeps stealing glances at you," Zovi said playfully to Cove.

"Oh yeah, that boy got a little lovestruck," Cove said, laughing. "He's cute though. What's his strength?"

"He's pretty skilled in parkour, but he's well-rounded, so he says," Zovi said. "He caught on to surfing pretty quickly yesterday, and that was a good testament to his proficiency picking up new sports."

Cove nodded at Zovi's words. "Well, we'll see. I'm happy living a single life. But if he makes power moves in my direction, I'll see then." She smiled, climbing into the leg press chair.

"What about Avior?" Cove asked Zovi.

"Well," Zovi said, choosing her words wisely. She wanted to be clear about the team's training but not reveal too much about the nature of Avior's imminent destiny. "He has an event coming up soon that requires a lot of different skills and disciplines combined together to accomplish a goal." Zovi thought for a second. "It's kind of a super, ultra, mega triathlon."

"Oh, word," Cove said, looking extremely impressed. "Okay, now that's awesome! I'm glad to be part of the team. That's an incredible goal." Cove returned her focus to her exercise, and Zovi shot a look at Avior, who, from across the dojo's space, caught her eye for a moment and nodded at her.

After a good warm-up, where each of the teammates touched base with every exercise machine, Kai called them over to the mixed martial arts cage. "Okay, kids, we are going to jump right into fighting today," he said. "I have an athlete here that has agreed to join me in a match." The four teammates looked startled at this news.

"You're going to fight?" Zovi asked, looking concerned.

"Yes," Kai said solidly. "I'm going to show you all why I am the coach." There was a force in his voice that they had not heard before.

Just then, the athlete Kai had been speaking to earlier came out of the men's locker room and walked toward them. He was built like a tank. Every muscle rippled with each step. He had a shaved head and was not smiling whatsoever. "This is Dallas Dietrich. He is a professional UFC fighter. We are going to commence into a full contact fight as soon as I put my grappling gloves on."

"Holy...," Midas said in a hushed voice as he sized up the situation. Kai slid his grappling gloves on and strapped them tight. Dallas climbed into the cage and bounced on his toes as he shrugged his shoulders and shook his large arms.

"You ready?" Dallas asked in a husky voice.

"Three, two, one, go," Kai said steadily. The two fighters tapped gloves, then sprang into action. Dallas let loose a vicious kick to Kai's leg. Kai took the kick, then muscled forward and feinted with his left arm while his right punched Dallas in the ribs. Dallas didn't even flinch. He threw a gunslinger right at Kai's head. Kai blocked, threw his own right jab, and then whipped around on the spot with a round-house kick. Dallas got his arm up to block, but the kick was strong and still knocked hard on the side of his head. Dallas got a left punch into Kai's stomach, then grabbed onto his head and maneuvered into a choke hold. In an amazing burst of energy that was surprising for a man of Kai's age, he reached over his head, grabbed hold of Dallas's head, and backflipped up out of the choke hold, landed behind him, and slugged him hard as concrete in the back of the head. Dallas's lights went out like a switch, and, knocked out cold, he fell forward face-first flat onto the mat of the ring.

"OHHHHHH!" yelled Avior, Zovi, Midas, and Cove.

"Piece of cake," Kai said, barely even breathing hard. "Soon as he comes to, what do you guys say about inviting Dallas to join our team?"

"Yeah, all right, sounds fine to me," Avior said, looking at the unconscious spartan-physique form in front of him.

"Well, shoots, he barely lasted thirty seconds with you, Kai!" Midas said loudly. "How good is he?"

"Just because the bout was short doesn't mean he's not skilled. I'm not sure how to impress upon you all the level that I operate at without potentially scaring you." Avior, Zovi, Midas, and Cove looked suddenly at Kai in a new light at these words. With a playful wave of his hand, Kai dismissed the seriousness of the moment.

One groggy awakening later and Dallas was back on his feet, massaging the back of his head. "Dallas, we are in the middle of a training spree where we touch base and become proficient in a multitude of different disciplines. Would you be interested in running parallel with our team as we train? I can offer you coaching expertise that you will not find anywhere else," Kai said as he held out his hand to Dallas. Dallas frowned, clearly a little resentful that he had been bested so quickly, but slowly took Kai's hand and shook it.

"I could use some fresh skills," Dallas said with a bit of what sounded like a Tennessee twang in his voice. "Y'all look like a fit bunch. If I come out better than before, that's all I want." The four friends nodded and became five.

"All right, it's settled then. Welcome to the team, Dallas," Kai said, snapping back to business. "Avior, step forward," he continued. Avior did so. "Strap on these grappling gloves. You are going to fight Zovi, Midas, and Cove, back-to-back-to-back." Startled, Avior swung his gaze from Kai to Zovi. Zovi looked shocked, but then, as Kai handed her a pair of grappling gloves, her gaze hardened. Avior winced at the thought of punching Zovi's beautiful face. He knew though that if he was going to become tough enough to face the obstacles inside the Interverse, he had to follow Kai's commands. "Enough standing around! Midas, Cove, get ready! If Avior gets Zovi into submission or knocks her out, Midas, you're in! Cove, you'll follow after Midas. Avior," Kai put his head right in front of Avior's face, so close that nobody else could hear what he was saying, "you damn well better win this thing if you want to stand any chance at what your future holds."

"Three! Two! One! Go!" Kai bellowed. Avior knew to his core he had to win this three-part fight. He let absolute fury flood into his heart. Zovi was moving toward him. She looked as if she was about to kill him by the look on her face. She seemed to have buckled down her emotions as well. Avior raised his hands, shielding his head, and stepped forward. He had never really fought before, but he instinctively knew how to fight for his life, and that's what kicked in. Zovi aggressively threw a mean left-right-left combo at his head. Avior blocked two of the punches while the third hit him on the cheekbone. He lunged forward on his left leg, ramming his right knee into Zovi's stomach. She doubled over, then rolled sideways out of reach, stood up, caught her breath, and then swung a kick at Avior's head. He blocked. He let loose a barrage of punches at her torso. Some were blocked, and others made contact.

Zovi sidestepped then bear-clawed Avior on the ear with her hand. Avior grimaced, and at that moment, Zovi swept her right leg behind his legs and knocked him off his feet. She managed to get her arms around his neck and began to constrict his throat. Kai was about to start counting down to signal a pin when Avior did a lightning-quick abdominal crunch and thrust his knees up into Zovi's face. The impact was heavy, and Zovi lost her hold on Avior. They were both up on their feet in an instant. Zovi's lip was bleeding, and she had a black eye forming.

Avior still had two opponents to go; he needed to end this quickly and move on. He thought of how unfair it was that it was solely his responsibility to obtain this DNA sequence from the Interverse. His was a one-man mission with the fate of humanity hanging on his every move. He let his fury become a behemoth surge of berserker energy. He moved at Zovi and swung right, left, right, left, uppercut, bear claw swipe, high right kick, low left leg kick, then opened up into a relentless barrage of punches. Zovi was blocking what she could, but when he had kneed her in the face, she had gotten a little stunned. She was against the cage, her energy depleted. Avior knew he had her; he stood for a moment and looked at her. To his surprise, she winked and smiled. Her eyelids were heavy, and she was on the verge of fainting. Through her mouthguard, she whispered, "Do it."

Avior swung his right arm with all his might and knocked Zovi out cold. He stood stunned for a moment over her unconscious body. Suddenly a mighty blow struck him in the back of the head. Dazed, Avior turned quickly on the spot and faced Midas. He sized up Midas's stance in a second. In an epiphany, Avior realized that neither Midas nor Cove knew what was at stake with Avior's training. He smirked. They didn't know the level of fury that he had boiling inside him.

Avior moved confidently toward Midas. Midas was taken aback by the level of confidence with which Avior approached, but nonetheless, he squared up, ready for action. Avior threw a couple of blows just to get Midas, thinking of his forward space. In a split second, he sidestepped Midas and punched him in the ribs. Midas grunted, grabbing his ribs. Avior put his hands on Midas's back and forcefully rammed his right knee into Midas's exposed stomach. Midas grunted louder, doubled over, and held his stomach. Avior almost laughed. Midas, the parkour specialist, was all feather-footed and seemed to have little ability to inflict damage.

Avior darted behind Midas and wrapped his arms around his neck in a choke hold. Midas sputtered, gasping for breath, and clawed at Avior's arms. He pushed Avior backward until they smashed into the cage. Their feet got tangled up in the struggle, and they both slid down the wall of the cage and landed in a heap on the mat floor. Midas was punching Avior as best he could, but his strength was waning fast. Just as Midas was about to drift into unconsciousness, Kai dropped to his knee by the boy's side. "One! Two! Three! That's enough!" He shouted as he pulled Avior's arms off Midas's neck. Midas was on the edge of unconsciousness as Kai pulled him out of the cage.

Avior got to his feet and turned to look as Cove advanced menacingly toward him. He was tired, and his muscles were tight and aching, but he knew he had to defeat Cove. His eyes raked over her body, confirming what he already knew. Cove was an extremely adept athlete. Avior flexed his body, summoning energy from every atom of his being. Suddenly, a pitch-black orb the size of a quarter materialized out of the space right next to Avior's body. Cove shrieked when she saw the black orb and lost her focus. Avior hadn't seen the orb, and in a fraction of a second, he saw his moment. He sprinted forward and jumped completely horizontal in the air, feet first. He drop-kicked Cove with all his might. She slammed into the cage and got knocked out cold.

All the immense energy he had amassed from the fight was draining from him like someone had pulled his plug. Kai was bellowing from what seemed like a great distance away. Avior turned his head and saw that Kai, Zovi, Midas, and Dallas were all staring horror-struck at a point in space just over his shoulder. Turning his head, Avior came face-to-face with the pitch-black orb that was hovering a foot away. As he stared at it, he felt like he was staring into the infinite maw of a supermassive black hole. Whatever the orb was, it was draining Avior's energy like crazy. He felt like he could barely have lifted a toothpick. Head spinning, Avior collapsed, and his vision faded to black.

CHAPTER 5

LIPS MEET

Avior awoke from a dreamless sleep. He slowly lifted his eyelids and saw his arms folded gently on his chest in front of him. He was tucked into his bed in his condo in Waikiki. Opening his eyes further, he saw a crowd was gathered around him. Kai, Zovi, Midas, Cove, and Dallas were all looking worriedly at him as he came to. Avior saw that the doctor he had met when he had been recalled into his physical body was also among his teammates.

"Welcome back, Avior," the doctor said.

"Scary stuff man, scary stuff," Midas said with his forehead wrinkled in concern.

Zovi swooped in and softly hugged Avior, planting a delicate kiss on his cheek. "We were so worried…" she said trailing off as she stepped back from Avior.

Kai had a new steely look in his eye as he surveyed Avior, but he managed a smile. Cove and Dallas were looking shocked and perplexed.

"I'm afraid we have a new obstacle, Avior," the doctor said, getting straight to the point. Midas, Cove, and Dallas were confused. They still didn't have the faintest clue as to what Avior was going through. "We ran some tests on you while you were unconscious. By the way, it's been a full day that you've been out cold," the doctor said as he stood by Avior's bedside table. The doctor had that same intelligent twinkle of supreme hope glowing in his eyes that he had had upon first telling Avior of his destiny. His eyes reassured Avior.

Kai held out a hand to stop the doctor. "Three of my teammates don't know Avior's mission," he said. The doctor turned to the others. "I'll make this concise and to the point then. The particle constituents of Avior's body can align in such a way that they tune into the fabric of reality of a space that we are calling the *Interverse*." The doctor paused, letting that information sink in. "It is very possible that Avior can be a vessel between these two spaces, and, in accordance with the properties of the nature of this 'Interverse,' there is the chance that he can generate a strand of DNA from there that we can utilize to benefit humanity in endless advantageous ways. That strand is the Omniscript."

Midas, Cove, and Dallas stared awestruck at Avior. A long moment of silence passed as the three absorbed this news. The doctor straightened up. "As I was saying, this newest obstacle poses a difficult challenge. After running tests on your body, we discovered that you were attacked by a living being that resembles the same kind of natural forces that make up a black hole." The doctor looked grave. Zovi looked distraught. Everybody's shoulders sank at this. "The kind of energy output required of you, Avior, is also the kind of energy that attracts these beings. They feed on pure energy. If I had to guess, they are most similar to jellyfish. Mindless beings that operate on pure reflex and are attracted to copious amounts of energy. It seems your bout in the ring semiphased your body into Interverse space, causing one of these black hole beings to come through." The doctor made a soothing gesture. "The being has dissipated. They may only live for mere moments. But when the time comes for you to put all your training together and go forth into the Interverse, I am terribly sorry to inform you that they will be a concerning factor for you to deal with."

Avior grimaced as he moved his body in his bed. "Do you think there's any way to combat these beings? Or should I just avoid them at all costs?" Avior asked the doctor.

"Black holes are infinite, invincible forces of nature. As far as I know, these beings are as well. I would recommend you run for your life when you come across one. One alone will drain you to unconsciousness, but a group could, potentially, kill you," the doctor said seriously. "And Avior, we may never have another like you. You are our only hope of obtaining the Omniscript."

Avior nodded, "Well, at least now I know to bolt for it next time I come across one of these black hole beings."

"Yes," the doctor said, giving Avior that ever-hopeful look. "Well, I bid you all adieu. I must be off. My colleagues and I are deep diving our research continuously these days." The doctor fixed Avior with a final friendly, smiling look. "Avior," he said with a curt nod, then departed.

"Okay, so, I'm mind-blown," Midas said. Cove and Dallas murmured in agreement.

"Then you understand why we cannot broadcast Avior's mission to the world," Kai said. "I was reluctant to let you three in on that information, but Avior could really use the best support possible from his teammates."

Cove looked at Avior seriously, her usual rambunctious pluckiness turned down. "Avior, we are with you one hundred percent," she said. "I'll be the best training partner that I can be. And no hard feelings for that dropkick you gave me," she winked but kept a straight face.

Dallas ran his hand over his shaved head, "Bro, that's a heavy journey you're on. This is like the mission of all missions. Same as what Cove said, I'll be the best teammate ever for you, man."

Zovi came over to Avior's bed and sat down, putting her arm around his shoulder. "Well, I'm glad we're all on the same page now. I guess if we acquire more teammates in the future, we should break the news right off the bat and get them on board." Kai nodded, then let his gaze drift gently out the window to the ocean view. "As Avior's personal trainer, I need to coach him through some stretches and easy exercises," Zovi said. "His body was almost completely drained of energy, and he needs to coerce it back into gear."

Midas, Cove, and Dallas nodded and headed out of Avior's bedroom. Kai's gaze returned from the ocean view to Avior. "Zovi will help you recuperate," he said. "We will wait until your body is ready before we recommence training. But don't take too long," he said with a steely glint in his eye. "We're on a deadline, remember? You only have one full Interverse phase in you, and the longer we wait, the harder it will be to sustain it." With that, Kai placed his large hand on Avior's shoulder, then left the condo.

Zovi was still sitting on Avior's bed. Avior's heart was beating a little faster than usual. She was looking at his face closely, reading his features. "How are you feeling?" she asked, her eyes fixed on his.

"Fatigued," he said, allowing his eyes to move over her face.

She looked genuinely worried. "You don't know how scary it was to see that black hole being appear out of the space around you and eat all your energy. I mean, that thing is a straight-up alien! It's like a bomb blew up in my mind when I saw it. A creature from an intersecting universe that eats energy! Geez, what a nightmare," she said. "And then once you fell on your back and passed out, your eyes were all rolled back in your head, and your posture kind of shriveled up. It was awful to watch," Zovi said with teary eyes as she shared her vision of the scene with Avior.

"And now think, once you make your phase shift into the Interverse, you're going to have to deal with potentially running into those things everywhere you go. What if you get trapped in a group of them and you can't escape?" she said, holding on to Avior's arm. "Gosh, I don't even want to continue that train of thought," she went on. Collecting herself, Zovi barged forward. "We're just going to have to train you so incredibly well that you can operate on the edge of a dime." She sighed deeply, looking out of the window at the blue horizon. "Well, let's start right now on getting you recuperated.

They started slowly. Zovi helped Avior out of bed and got him to lie on a mat on the floor. "I'm going to help you stretch your muscles. As you stretch, I'll massage the muscles to coax them back into action. We need to encourage blood circulation and oxygen flow through your body. You got locked up pretty bad back there," Zovi said as she straightened Avior's legs and began kneading his muscles with her hands. Avior was in a bad state. His body was as rigid as a board from being drained of all his energy. Breathing was tough, with only short breaths possible.

"What was it like?" Zovi asked. "You know, when that black hole being was draining you?" Avior looked up at the ceiling as she kneaded his quad muscle.

"It felt like dying, I guess. All my vigor just disappeared," Avior said with a frown. "I know the doctor said that they're like jellyfish, you know, mindless creatures of reflex. But I could feel its presence, like when someone is staring at you really hard."

Zovi's forehead rose in surprise. She turned her head from her work to look at Avior. "If that's what their jellyfish can do, imagine what kinds of other creatures may exist in the Interverse."

Avior groaned. "Frick, I didn't think about that." He grinned. "Let's be optimistic though. Maybe that's all there is out there," he said hopefully.

Zovi let a little smile show. "Well, best we can do is get you trained to the point that you can handle anything."

Avior nodded, "Agreed."

Zovi moved her hands to Avior's arms and began kneading and massaging his biceps and fore-arms. Avior relaxed, allowing Zovi to work her exper-tise on him. His legs certainly felt better now. With the rhythm of stretching and muscle massaging, his breath had lengthened, and his lungs felt like they were filling all the way up with air. Avior noticed that every now and then, only for a moment, Zovi's pro-fessionalism would falter, and she seemed to touch him with loving hands. Avior's gaze fixed on Zovi's face. She was busy working, but she was blushing, and she was avoiding his gaze.

"You know, however this mission turns out, what's next for you?" Avior asked. Zovi's focus stayed on her work, but she pondered for a minute. "Well, I suppose I'll connect with my next athlete. I'd like to help at least a handful of top athletes before I pursue further school and later my career." She looked over at Avior's face, a hint of blush still on her cheeks. "But this is it. This journey we're all on with you as you strive to obtain the Omniscript, this is it. If we can get it, it's going to revolutionize so many things." She moved her hands to Avior's pecs and began massaging the muscle.

She was looking hopefully at Avior, and he could see his own face reflected in her eyes. With the thought of how he had nearly died, and how his odds of perishing had just skyrocketed with the discovery of the black hole beings, he felt a primal surge in his core. Avior reached his right arm up and grabbed Zovi's head from the back and pulled her toward him. Their lips met with a strong plush force. Avior's eyes were closed; his lips fully savoring the feel of Zovi against him. Zovi's eyes were wide with surprise, but her eyes soon fluttered as she sank into the kiss.

Avior moved his left hand from Zovi's shoulder to the small of her back. He had never kissed a girl before, either in the Simulation or here, in the real world. Their lips moved blissfully over each other. The chemistry was effervescent, the electricity, precious. Avior was kissing Zovi like a soldier going to war, and Zovi was letting all her pent-up feelings for Avior pour forth.

After many kiss-filled minutes of pure heaven, Zovi propped herself on her arms over Avior and looked down at him smiling. "What are we going to do about this?" She was smiling wider than Avior had ever seen her smile.

Avior solidly winked and returned a loving smile. "Well, there's no rule book about all this. At worst, Kai's going to scold us for being unprofessional."

"But do you think us having open feelings for each other is going to interfere with our training?" Zovi asked sincerely.

"If anything, us having open feelings is a massive benefit to our training," Avior said seriously. "It's been just me all my life. I feel like now that I've expressed my feelings for you to you, I have something to fight for. I'm not too sure the proper way to say this, but do you want to go out with me? You know, we can be a little team of two inside Kai's team as we go forward. I don't want to hide my feelings for you because if I go into the Interverse and I don't return, I want to know that I have no regrets and I didn't hold anything back."

Zovi listened intently to Avior's words and thought it all through for a moment. Finally she smiled, and with a gorgeous flutter of her eyes, she leaned in and kissed Avior deeply. They savored the fire of passion that blazed with their kiss. After a long quiet moment that was filled with only the sound of lips moving across lips, Zovi rolled over to lie beside Avior on the mat on his bedroom floor. "That's a yes," Zovi said cheekily. Avior smiled at the ceiling and reached over to hold her hand. The sun shone softly through the window as the ocean rolled endlessly on along the Waikiki shoreline.

"Honestly, I feel a lot better," Avior said, turning his head to the side to look at Zovi. "Physically, mentally, spiritually, emotionally. Physically, the muscle massage coaxed some circulation back into my body. Mentally, finally finding the moment to just go for it and make a move on you cleared my mind so much. And spiritually, now that I've professed my feelings for you to you, my spirit feels like a crystalline shining beacon of light pointing into this massive future." Avior moved his gaze from Zovi's right eye to her left. "And emotionally, kissing you and looking into those diamond eyes you have…"

Zovi giggled and nodded. "I know, same.

"What do you think about the next training challenge?" Zovi asked.

"Well…I might be ready, what is it? Do you know?" Avior said.

"Kai wants us all to bike all the way around the island," Zovi said earnestly. "It's about 130 miles, give or take. What are you feeling? I know you need to rest and recuperate, but your window of time is narrowing."

Avior inhaled deeply, then exhaled, "I think after a good night's sleep, I should be good to go. I might be a little rusty, but once I warm up and get moving, I should be all right. You can tell Kai that your work on me today was a success and that I'm back in action."

Zovi got to her feet excitedly. "Awesome! Avior, I think you're just the best. You know that, right?"

Avior chuckled. "Thanks, you're pretty swell yourself."

Zovi reached out her hand, and Avior reached up and grabbed it. She helped Avior up off the mat and embraced him warmly. "Well, I better get going. I'll tell Kai you're good to go. We'll all be over here tomorrow morning, bikes and all. Should be fun!"

Avior let his eyes drink Zovi up, head to toes. "Good night, Zovi. Thanks for today. I wouldn't be the way I am without you," he said.

Zovi clasped her hands and gave him a loving look. Avior stepped in and gave her a soft peck on the lips, holding her chin for a moment. She giggled as he pulled away, then tossed a shaka at him with her hand, flung back her blonde hair, and swooshed out of Avior's bedroom, making her way home. Avior went to bed that night with the biggest smile on his face, his lips still glossy from the lip balm Zovi had been wearing.

BIKE THE ISLAND

Avior awoke after a deep sleep feeling on top of the world. His dream state drifted smoothly into conscious thoughts with Zovi's face at the forefront of his mind. He made his bed, dressed into an athletic outfit, cleaned up, and then checked his phone. He had a missed call from Kai. Just as Avior was about to call him back, a knock sounded at the door.

"Yo! Avior! We're all downstairs! You better be ready!" Midas's kid-next-door voice carried through the door.

Avior smiled and went to open the door. "I'm up, I'm up! I'm ready, let's go," Avior said as he swung the door back to reveal a grinning Midas.

"Yo, glad to see you're back on top," Midas said as he looked at Avior's chipper face. Zovi was still swimming in Avior's vision, and something in his eyes gave him away. "Wow, what's got into you? You're all lovey-dovey'd up this morning," Midas commented as he saw Avior's eyes.

Avior winked but decided he'd wait for the right moment to break the news about his budding romance with Zovi. "Oh, I just had some great dreams last night," Avior said offhandedly. Midas looked a little dubious but punched Avior's shoulder, and they headed down the hall to the elevator.

Outside Kai was standing proudly in the parking lot with the team around him. Everyone had shiny new road bikes. "A generous contribution to our efforts from the doctors!" Kai exclaimed, gesturing at the brand-new expensive-looking bikes.

"How ya feeling, Avior?" Zovi called from beside Kai, with a massive smile spread across her beautiful face. Avior couldn't help but let his eyes drink her in deeply, but he snapped into his professional mode as it was time to gear up for serious training. "Tip-top shape. I'm definitely ready to hit the streets!" he said.

As Avior sidled up next to Kai and Zovi, he noticed Midas spitting some game at Cove as he handed her an energy bar for her backpack. Cove was chuckling at Midas as he rambled on in his neighborhood-kid sort of way, but she took the energy bar and was clearly enjoying Midas's power moves. Dallas was even tossing a couple of flirtatious lines at Cove when Midas would turn his head. Avior smiled to himself. The aloha spirit of the islands was the perfect kindling for puppy love. He caught Zovi's eye and saw her twinkling gaze lingering on him.

"All right! Let's all finish prepping and get a move on!" Kai said with his commanding coach voice.

Dallas gave Cove one last cheeky look then swung his bike up near Kai. "I really want this extreme cardio we've got today. You can bet your bottom dollar I'll be near the front," he said solidly.

Kai nodded his affirmative. Kai and Dallas were more physical people than social and shared many silent curt head nods between conversations with other people.

"Let's go! Follow me!" Kai shouted. Kai, Zovi, Avior, Midas, Cove, and Dallas started pedaling and rode their bikes out of the parking lot of Avior's condo building and onto Kalakaua Avenue. "We've got crazy Waikiki first, so stay tight. There's lots of traffic and wild pedestrians through here," Kai shouted over his shoulder at everyone.

Avior turned on his razor-sharp focus, but Zovi cruised over to his side, and he felt waves of love wash over him. "Hey there, tiger," she said just loud enough for him to hear, "we can train strong today, but stick by me. I wanna make sure you don't push yourself too hard. Your body isn't at one hundred percent yet, and you need to stay within reason on the training today."

Avior looked sideways at her. He really, truly appreciated her. She was so determined to keep him well at all times, in so many ways. Avior nodded at her, noticing how cute and funny she looked with a big bicycle helmet on her head. "Sounds good, at least

Kai doesn't have us fist fighting again today. That was a humongous barrier I had to break, to fight you the last time we trained."

Zovi grimaced. "I know, but it was a necessary step. Kai wants to break down all the barriers that are containing you. You need to be able to go nuclear when the time arises."

Avior knew that was true. He looked at the back of Kai's head. Kai had a pedal-to-the-metal approach to moving forward with training. Avior sighed. But Kai was able to console people when the going got tough. And his words always spurred Avior to step forward into new unknown realms that he had not previously thought about.

Avior glanced around as they sped through the streets of Waikiki. Midas was pumping his legs in a good rhythm with his tongue poking out between his teeth in concentration. Cove had set her phone on a bracket on her bike and was choosing a song to listen to through her earbuds. Dallas was beside Kai in the front of the pack, silently plowing forward. Avior chuckled. Dallas, who had seemed one of the most eager to receive the expertise of Kai's coaching, was making a point to move every muscle of his body as he rode to ensure a full-body workout. Avior laughed at Dallas's funny spectacle in front of him as his whole bodybuilder form shimmied as he rode.

"Great start, everyone!" Kai shouted over his shoulder. "The trick is to find your rhythm and synch your breathing to that!" At his words, the whole team noticeably started clicking into each of their rhythms.

Waikiki was a blast to bike through, Avior thought. The shops, the sky-rises, the aroma of restaurants, the magic of myriads of people milling through the beach streets. It was eye candy all the way.

Avior pulled up next to Kai, who was leading the pack with Dallas off to his other side. "So, we're going to wrap clockwise around the island?" Avior asked.

"Yep! Don't worry. We are going to take breaks every thirty miles, and we'll have a nice lunch somewhere. It's the cardio that counts, and trust me, we're all getting plenty of that today," Kai said, smiling as he glanced over at Avior.

With Kai leading the team, they all made their way through Waikiki, then cruised through Aiea, swooped through Pearl City, raced along the streets of Waipahu, and then blasted down the avenues of Kapolei, where they pulled over into a shady park for a break.

"Everybody okay?" Kai asked as the team dismounted their bikes in the shade of the trees at the park.

"All good!" the team sounded in unison.

"Good, good. Okay, I want a quick rundown from each of you," Kai said.

"Zovi?"

"I feel fine," Zovi replied. "I'm sticking near to Avior to ensure he's not experiencing anything out of the ordinary that may still be lingering from the other day."

"Excellent. And Avior? What's the report?" Kai asked.

"I was a little tight off the start, but once I found my rhythm, everything fell into place."

"That's my boy," Kai said, praising Avior's toughness despite his rough past couple of days.

"Midas?" Kai asked, looking over at Midas, who was chewing an energy bar and swigging a sports drink.

"Killing it!" Midas said through a mouthful of food and drink. Cove chuckled at Midas.

Kai smiled. "And little Miss Treasure Trove? Cove, how're you doing?"

Cove faced her chuckles to the sky and squinted. "Oh, baby, my legs are burning! But my booty is getting in shape!"

Kai guffawed while Midas and Dallas gave Cove cheeky glances. "And my fierce fighter! Mr. Dallas Dietrich, how ya holdin' up?"

Dallas pounded a fist into an open palm and nodded. "Just keepin' on, keepin' on," he said proudly.

"Boom, sounds good," Kai said with his hands on his hips. "Everybody grab a quick bite, hydrate, and stretch it out just a little. We need to be on our way."

The team did just that, and, after a rejuvenating break, they were all back on their bikes and blazing off up the street out of the shade of the trees in the park.

They wound their way around the last of the south side of the island and then started to make their way up the west coast. They muscled up through Nanakuli, passing the regal mountains and serene beaches, then pedaled their way northward through Waianae. The sea breeze felt heaven-sent on their skin in the tropical sun. Occasionally someone would put on a spurt of speed, and the order of their lineup would change as one person overtook another. They reached the northwest end of the paved road and shot intrepidly onto the dirt road that leads to Ka'ena Point State Park.

What a joy it was, Avior thought, *to be away from the cars and towns.* They pedaled their way on the rugged road around the breathtaking landscape around them. They had the sea to their left, the mountains to their right, and the fire of their camaraderie burning as they muscled onward together.

They rounded the northwest corner of the island at Ka'ena Point, then shot straight along the quiet coast for another few miles before Kai slowed to a roll and pulled off the shoulder of the road into the shade of a grove. "Second break! Everybody, you know the drill, grab a bite, hydrate, stretch it out, and socialize a little bit to bring your minds out of their internal mode back into the world for a minute," Kai said stoutly with his commanding coach voice. The team clambered off their bikes, thankful for the break, and began taking snacks and drinks out of their backpacks.

Zovi grabbed her water bottle and a bag of trail mix, then strode confidently over to Avior and looped her arm through his. Avior's eyebrows raised;

he was still a little nervous about public displays of affection, especially since Kai was right there. Avior wasn't sure how Kai would react when he inevitably caught on to the budding romance he had with Zovi. Zovi looked at Avior warmly. She seemed unfazed by these concerns.

"How ya holdin' up there, tiger?" she asked with a cute inflection in her voice.

"Honestly, I feel good. My muscles are rippling like crazy, but I've got today's training in the bag, for sure," Avior said, looking down at Zovi's sun-flushed face. Out of the corner of his eye, Avior saw Kai take notice of Zovi's arm through his. But, with a smirk and wink, Kai turned back to his conversation with Dallas. He wasn't sure what he had been expecting from Kai about Zovi, but at least, it wasn't a scolding or, worse, removal of Zovi from the team.

Still a little unsure of how to go about showing his affection for Zovi in front of the others, he kept a straight back when talking to her, only softly saying how pretty she looked standing there in the grove when no one was paying attention to them. After a suitable amount of time, in which everyone was able to rejuvenate themselves, and Kai gave Avior another side-eye glance with a knowing twinkling wink, his commanding coach voice boomed out, "All right, team, we've got a nice serene stretch all the way across the north shore. Our next pit stop is over on the east side in Kaaawa by the beach. Let's get a move on."

The legendary north shore stretch was beyond beautiful. Lush countryside curved around by bays and beaches teeming with happy people. Avior liked seeing all the people as they played blissfully on the serene shores. They reminded him of what he was training for. If he could get the Omniscript, this beautiful life would be improved by a hundredfold. The Omniscript could potentially slow aging, per- haps bring it near to a halt. People could live spry young lives many times as long as presently possible. Genetics could be perfected, allowing everybody born to be in stellar shape, potentially even completely rid- ding the world of birth defects and other disabilities. The doctors had even mentioned advancing human evolution. How cool would that be to have genetic superpowers! Avior looked skyward, deep in thought. *Maybe one day he could have an absolute Olympian of a child of his own.*

Avior looked sideways at Zovi. She was concen- trating on the road in front of her, but she noticed him in her peripheral vision and looked over at him. They shared a loving look for a long moment. Suddenly everything happened at once. Another bicyclist shot around a corner and whipped in next to them. His turn scared a rooster off the grass, and it ran out into the street, right in front of Midas. Midas yanked his handlebars left, then right, trying to avoid the crowing rooster. Midas's hands slipped off his handlebars, and he lost control and careened across the road. Not missing a beat, the other bicyclist shot across the street after him. Midas hit the guardrail and flipped over his handlebars, sliding through the grass, which to the team's horror had death-drop-cliff feet from where Midas was sliding. The bicyclist dove off his bike and did a baseball side-slide behind Midas, grabbing him by his collar.

Midas screamed and fell off the cliff. The bicyclist managed to grab a handhold on a rock and, with a wrench, came to a painful stop on the cliff's precipice, holding Midas by his collar above the death drop. "GET HIM!" Kai bellowed. Avior was there in an instant, wrapping his hands around the bicyclist's arm.

"I NEED HELP!" Avior yelled. Kai, Zovi, Cove, and Dallas were by him just in time. Midas's shirt was ripping, and his face was contorted in terror as his wide eyes stared horror-struck down at the jagged rocks below. Avior lifted the bicyclist with all his might, and with the entire team there grabbing Avior, they created enough anchorage in the slick grass to heave the bicyclist and Midas back up over the top of the cliff.

Midas was on all fours, his shirt barely intact, a nightmarish look on his face. He vomited on the grass. The bicyclist was shaking and looking scared out of his wits. "Everybody, move away from the cliff! Now!" Kai yelled. Cove helped Midas to his feet, and the group moved away from the cliff, back across the street to their bikes. "Over here." Kai motioned to the grass by the bikes. "Everybody, sit down." Still shaking, everyone took a seat in the grass. "Okay, let's get hold of the situation," Kai said sternly, looking in turn at everyone. "What's your name, young man?" Kai asked the bicyclist.

"Yelangelo Yarborough," the bicyclist said, taking off his helmet to reveal a head full of big thick dreadlocks.

"Are you a local?" Kai asked.

"Just moved here from Senegal, Africa," the young man said with his scared face slowly relaxing into relief. The team nodded at the midnight-skinned African, murmuring their thanks.

"I am so sorry, my man," Yelangelo said to Midas. "I did not see that rooster. That was a very unfortunate situation."

Midas's eyes were closed. He nodded, then collapsed in the grass.

"I'm not even going to think twice about asking you this," Kai said severely, "We could use you on our team. This is me recruiting you right here and now. Train with us. That save was beyond proof of your prowess and courage. You will be compensated at the conclusion of your time with this team."

Yelangelo looked around at Avior, Zovi, Midas, Cove, and Dallas. He started, "What are you training for? Some kind…"

But Midas interrupted him from his position on the grass where he was still sprawled with his eyes closed, "That guy," he pointed vaguely at Avior, "is the savior of the universe, or something."

Yelangelo looked around at Avior. Everybody was staring at Yelangelo, silently conveying this truth. "Long story, but that's pretty much it," Dallas said aside to Yelangelo after a moment. Yelangelo took that information to heart and said no more.

Yelangelo joined the team, and with his simple and honest African nature, the team came together stronger than ever after Midas's narrow escape. They rode all the way across the north shore, made their way down the scenic east side, and late that afternoon rolled back into Waikiki. They were all a little subdued from the scare of the day, but Kai spoke up as they prepared to depart, "Team, our timeline is short. Avior, the doctors messaged me during our ride home. You have days before your ability to phase to the Interverse will disappear."

Yelangelo looked confused at these words but paid attention with a ready expression on his face. "We must push on," Kai continued. "Tomorrow, we will work on leg dexterity and power. We will smash out a soccer scrimmage match to warm up, then work on skateboarding. Everybody can skate, right?" Kai asked the team. Everybody nodded with various levels of vigor. Avior and Midas were great skaters, Zovi and Cove were amateurs, with Dallas looking a little unsure, and Yelangelo was asking, "Roller-skate?" The team laughed warmly, and Yelangelo smiled.

"Bright and early, you all know the drill," Kai said. "Great training today. Midas, you take a deep relaxing bath tonight."

Midas closed his eyes and nodded.

"Zovi, Cove, good work today. Zovi, thanks for keeping an eye on Avior," Kai said. Kai nodded at Zovi, then, lightning fast, so no one else saw, Kai flashed Avior a knowing look followed by a flicker of a wink. "Dallas, see you tomorrow. Yelangelo, thank you for that save today, glad you're onboard. And Avior," Kai said pointedly to Avior, "we're almost there." He smiled. "You're doing fantastic, kid." He turned for his truck, "Boom. See you all tomorrow." The team was thankful to have the tail end of the afternoon to relax, and everyone slowly started departing. As Avior started to make his way back to his building, Zovi slipped in front of him and gave him a puckered-up smooch on the lips, then slapped his butt with a laugh and made her way home.

CHAPTER 7

LEG SHRED SESSION

Everybody slept like logs and awoke feeling ready for their skate session. Kai picked the team up in his truck, and when Avior, who was standing out in the parking lot of his condo, saw the jam-packed truck pull up, he broke out laughing.

"Ho! You like one party truck, Mr. Universe?" Cove cheekily joked as the truck slowed to a stop beside Avior.

"Yeah, hop in! We're playing Twister back here!" Midas said loudly with windswept hair and tears of joy in his eyes. Avior noticed that Midas had a renewed appreciation for life after his nearly dying the day before.

"Jump in, babe," Zovi said. Avior was surprised; she was openly loving on him in front of the team, who were all now smirking at him.

"It's all in the clear, my bro," Dallas said, smiling from his reclined position in the bed of the truck. "That girl told us how straight twitterpated she is for you."

Avior turned his head to look at Zovi. "I couldn't help it," she said slyly with a wide smile. "I had to get it off my chest."

Kai poked his head around Zovi with an understanding smile, "Can't say I didn't see it coming from a mile away," he chuckled. "And don't worry, you have my blessing. Every soldier going into battle needs a li'l love."

Relief swept over Avior. The world seemed so perfect right now. The shadow of his uncertain future was suddenly illuminated by his exposed heart, shining brightly for all to see. "You two can now say 'Nopp naa la' to each other," Yelangelo said with his earthy warmth. "It means 'I love you' in Wolof, my native language." Avior opened the passenger side door of the truck and squeezed in tightly next to Zovi. They looked at each other, with everybody clustered around all googly-eyed.

"Nopp naa la," Avior said, looking Zovi in the eyes.

"Nopp naa la," she replied, the nearby ocean reflecting in her eyes as she gazed into Avior's depths.

"Noppy nally, noppy nally, let's go already!" Midas said happily, clapping Avior on the back through the little window between the truck's cab and the bed.

They arrived at Kamilo'iki Park after a morale-boosting, sun-soaked, ocean-side drive up the coast. Everybody was in superhigh spirits as they all clambered out of Kai's truck. "All righty, we're going to do a warm-up soccer scrimmage to get some leg dexterity into your muscles," Kai said, sizing up the sizable soccer field by the skate park. Everybody looked sharkishly at each other. Apparently everybody was good at soccer.

"How about Avior, Zovi, and Yelangelo on one team. And we'll have Midas, Cove, and Dallas on the other," Kai directed. "This is just a warm-up, no need to kill each other over the match. First to five wins." The two teams assembled and trooped onto the field. Kai stepped to the center and pulled a coin out of his pocket. "Avior?" he asked.

"Heads," Avior replied.

Kai flipped the coin, caught it, and slapped it to his forearm. "Tails. Midas, Cove, Dallas, you three get kickoff," Kai said and stepped off the field.

The game was quick and high-spirited. Everybody was still waking up, and kicking the soccer ball around got their minds moving and their legs warmed. The girls surprised the boys with their expert-level skills. Zovi and Cove had very nimble feet and were able to snake their way adroitly through the boys. Yelangelo, however, had spent a lot of time in the back fields of Africa playing soccer in crude conditions. He was a shockingly adept player and blasted a couple of scorching hotshots for scores. Thanks to this, Avior, Zovi, and Yelangelo won the warm-up match and sauntered comically over to Kai with grins above their chins.

"Nice, nice, nice," Kai said, smiling. "Don't swagger around so hard just yet. I want to see focused training out of you all today. I know we have a couple of you that are skilled and a couple that are a little on the novice side. Today's skateboarding is about working leg power, eye-to-foot coordination, and body control. It is *not* a competition. I want you all to play nicely together and work as hard as you can. Avior, I remember seeing you absolutely shredding in the Simulation. I expect nothing less than that today," Kai said, giving Avior his stern coach stare, but then his expression softened into smiling eyes. "Enough chitchat, get in there!" he boomed.

The team all grabbed their boards from the truck bed and strolled smoothly into the Kamilo'iki skate park. As they entered, three skaters were in the process of leaving. "Nice line, Ionakana!" a pretty red-haired girl said to the guy beside her.

"Thanks, Satellite! You and Isla did great in there," Ionakana said happily. The three departing skaters acknowledged Avior and the team, then made their way across the park to the bus stop. Now that the team was in the skate park, Yelangelo and Dallas looked a little unsure of themselves. "I am from dirt roads…" Yelangelo said, his voice trailing off as he looked around.

Dallas looked at Yelangelo. "Bruh, I am a straight gym rat. I'm going to fall right on my muscly butt," he said.

Zovi and Cove had already taken off across the park to the quarter pipes and were pumping back and forth. Avior and Midas were standing next to Yelangelo and Dallas and exchanged sharkish smirks. "Well, I'm right at home on my board," Midas said casually, nodding.

Avior eyed the park confidently and then said, "If my brain carries over my skateboarding skill from the Simulation, and I hope it does, I may be about to absolutely destroy this park today."

Midas laughed out loud.

A short Japanese boy swerved past them and dropped in. He was wearing subtle earth tone clothes with loudly colored skate shoes, and atop his head was the most perfect bowl-cut hairstyle. He tre-flipped the euro gap, swung around, popped a clean backside flip on the bank of the pyramid, and then rolled over and executed a kickflip-blunt-kickflip-out on the coping of the quarter pipe.

"Sheeeesh! Nice one, yeah!" Midas shouted out at him.

Avior nodded, impressed. He glanced over at Kai. Kai had his eyes on the Japanese boy; then with a smile, his head turned to look at Avior, and he nodded. Avior threw his board down and dropped in. He pumped around the entire park, prepping his legs. He launched out of a pocket and coasted toward a ledge. *Here we go*, he thought, as he approached the ledge. With surprising ease, he popped an ollie and clipped into a buttery frontside tail slide. The Simulation glimmered in his eyes as all his digital skills kicked in. He slid several feet, then flicked his foot out, kicking a kickflip out of the tailslide that snapped back underneath his shoes. With a thud, he landed bolts, surprised at how flawlessly his Simulation abilities had carried over into the real world. The team cheered from their spots around the park.

Avior leaned forward and pushed off. He turned around the edge of the park and approached the flat bar rail. With a quick crouch, he popped an ollie into a backside smith grind. He held the grind across the entire rail; then with a smooth movement, he popped a back one-eighty out of his backside smith. "Yeah, you!" Midas shouted as Avior rolled past him, now in a switch stance. Avior rolled straight toward a slope, which looked to be about the size of an eight stair. He relaxed and took a breath, and with his palms open, he flicked a fluid switch flip through the air down the slope. Bolts.

Kai cheered enthusiastically from his spot by the fence. Avior could tell Kai had really been praying that Avior's Simulation abilities would carry over without a hitch or a glitch. Avior looked up and thanked the sky, happy that that was the case. "Yeah, Avior!" Zovi shrieked, skating over. She bumped up against him and kissed his cheek, ruffling his hair a little with her hand.

"My turn!" Midas called out loudly. He dropped in, shooting straight for the euro gap. With a flourish, he laser heeled the euro, landed squarely on his board, and then immediately popped a backslide heel.

"All right! All right!" Cove said, clapping and laughing at Midas's sprightly style, which had an exaggerated swagnificence to it. Midas continued, now in switch stance, and made a line over to the pocket, where he went up and then pumped back down, gaining speed. He moved his feet into the fakie position; then with gentle grace, he flicked a nice slow fakie hard flip on the hip and caught it, stomping it back down on the bolts.

Yelangelo and Dallas were staring awestruck at the exhibition in front of them. Neither of them had seen skateboarding like this in person. Between the Japanese boy, Avior, and now Midas, they were getting quite the feast of tricks to enjoy. Cove climbed out of the quarter pipe, and without a second look took off toward the flat bar rail. She crouched, then popped an ollie into a nicely angled crooked grind. She came off the rail, then boosted down the slope toward the pyramid. She jetted up the bank of the pyramid then did a wall-ride up onto the metal coping of the top for a buttery fifty-fifty grind, then popped off back into the bank of the pyramid.

Zovi was right behind Cove. She dropped in on the slope, pumped the whole park, and then boosted up the corner pocket and shot back down toward the hip. She hucked a varial flip on the hip, landed it, and then rode up the slope and flicked a nollie varial flip. She landed it clean, then rolled backward off the slope. She moved her feet to a fakie, then hit the hip backward and kicked a fakie varial flip, making a trick trifecta of varial flips.

"Nice one, Zovi!" Kai called out from his spot by the fence. Avior rolled past Zovi and slid his hand across the small of her back, smiling at her technical prowess. Zovi looked pleased with herself as she grabbed her water bottle.

"All right, you two, get your butts in there and give it a shot!" Kai shouted across the park at Yelangelo and Dallas. They grinned at each other, then, one after the other, dropped in and pumped the park. They were wobbly and definitely looked like total rookies, but their determination paid off as they kept at it until they could pump the park with sure feet.

Avior still felt the urge to lay down something heavy, and with his brow furrowed, he dropped back in. The whole team watched in awe as Avior unleashed himself. One second he was nollie backside flipping off the top of the quarter pipe, and the next second, he was switch feeble grinding the flat bar rail. Avior was fully in his zone, landing trick after trick. The whole team, including the Japanese boy, could feel Avior's energy as he conquered obstacle after obstacle.

"Easy, Avior, easy!" Kai shouted out. Avior was so zoned in though, that he had tuned out everything. Avior knew he had it in him to lay down a trick that would forever be the trophy trick of the park. The team looked on, awestruck, as Avior stopped and walked in front of the biggest gap in the park. He was scoping the top of the tall pyramid, with the expanse of the whole bank that led up to its summit.

The gap was equivalent to about a fourteen stair, and Avior was fully prepared to conquer it. He rolled up to it once, to feel it out, then backed up and stared it down. Avior's presence was massive. His energy and concentration were at maximum. Kai was looking uneasy but knew Avior had to do what he had to do.

Without a word, Avior threw his board down and sped, in switch stance, at the enormous gap. He flexed every muscle in his taut body as he crouched, then, with a savage lunge, he popped off the top. Everybody's eyes were fixed on Avior as he threw a ferocious switch tre-flip off the top of the pyramid. The gravity of the moment was massive. Too massive. As if playing in slow motion, Avior came down from a textbook execution of his switch tre-flip, and as he approached the ground, the horrifying presence of a black hole being appeared from the fabric of Avior himself.

"NOOOO!" Zovi screamed, as Avior stomped the landing and saw the black hole being that was right on him.

"EVERYBODY, STAY PUT!" Kai bellowed. Avior could feel the overwhelming force upon him, pulling his energy out of his body.

Knowing nothing about what was going on, the Japanese boy sprang forward and shouted, "Turn yourself off! Sit down and enter Zen!"

Avior's mind was a tornado of energy leaving his body, but he complied and sat down midroll from his board and immediately pretended he was an inanimate object. He thought of the concrete, the park, nothingness, zero energy. The black hole being's pull on him lessened. Avior forced himself to be nothing. Just a closed pair of eyes above the clean concrete features. The black hole being sputtered as its energy feeding came to a halt. It flickered, then dissipated inches from Avior's left temple.

"Good lord, boy, how on earth did you know to tell him that?" Kai asked the Japanese boy as he ran over to help Avior to his feet.

"I have no idea what that thing was," the Japanese boy said, "but I know what a black hole is, and that sure as day looked like one. I guess the logic of what to do just clicked in my head."

Kai nodded intensely; he was holding a shaking Avior under the arms as he helped him to his feet. "Ho, what is your name?" Avior asked the Japanese boy weakly.

"Ryuji Ryu," the Japanese boy said.

"Kai?" Avior asked Kai. Kai already knew what Avior meant.

"Ryuji, these teens here today are part of a training team I have assembled. We have only a short time left to train, but we sure could use those quick wits and tight tricks you have. Would you like to run with us for a while?" Kai asked Ryuji, still holding Avior.

"Well, I can't say I'm not curious as to what's going on, and I do love training, so okay. But what is going on?" he said.

Kai looked at Avior, then Ryuji. "This boy has a gift and a curse. Incredibly he has the potential to obtain a strand of DNA that could change the world.

The training we do as a team is what makes his chances of obtaining that DNA that much higher."

"And that black hole thing?" Ryuji asked.

"Dead on," Kai said. "It's some kind of a black hole being. Long story, but it exists in the same space that Avior exists in as well. Kai looked skyward, holding Avior. "That concludes our training for the day. We have one more challenge ahead of us before Avior must make his journey alone. Avior, do you think you are able to train tomorrow?"

Avior nodded, "It didn't get me too bad. I think I'll be okay. What do you have planned?"

Kai looked eastward with a squint. "Our final challenge is an outrigger canoe voyage from here, Oahu, across the channel to Maui. It will take a full day. And it will be grueling. But it is the final test to prepare you." Kai looked at everyone, slowly, in turn. "I am beyond grateful for each of you coming along with us as Avior prepares for what he must do. I think it would be best if everyone goes home and relaxes in preparation for tomorrow."

They all had steely glints in their eyes as they made their way out of the park and back to Kai's truck. Softly, so only Avior could hear, Zovi whispered, "Would you like me to stay with you tonight? Just to make sure you're all right?"

Avior furrowed his brow. "I really need to focus…"

Zovi put her hand in his. "I'll sleep in my sleeping bag," she said. "You need someone with you"—she looked into his eyes—"and that person is me.

And as your personal trainer, I believe it would be beneficial if you had company."

Avior felt relieved at Zovi's affection. He grinned. "Okay, but I really do need to start preparing my mind for what's coming soon."

"I promise I'll let you do that," Zovi said, "sooo, maybe just one kiss, or two, or a dozen."

Avior laughed, winking with the pain of the brief, but impactful, energy drain from the black hole being. Off in the distance, they heard Midas talking to Ryuji, "Ryuji Ryu, eh? Sounds like kangaroo. Can I call you *Kangaroo*?" Everybody, even Kai, laughed as they all piled into the truck and slowly drove off.

CHAPTER 8

ISLAND TO ISLAND

vior's alarm awoke him the next morning. It was long before dawn, but Kai wanted every-body prepared to depart by sunrise. Avior looked around and saw that Zovi had climbed from her sleeping bag into his bed sometime in the night. "The floor was too uncomfortable," Zovi murmured as she rubbed her eyes and rolled over. Avior sat for a moment, looking at her as she savored the last few moments of lying in bed. This was the first time he had ever seen a girl in bed with him. Her hair was tousled up, but it smelled like coconut shampoo. Her pajamas were a pair of track shorts and a little T-shirt that had a picture of ice cream on it. Avior smiled as he gazed at her.

Avior and Zovi cleaned up, grabbed their gear, had a snack, and then held hands as they made their way down the hall to the elevator. As they rode the elevator, they simply looked quietly at each other for a moment. There was a reassuring confidence reflecting between them. Avior wrapped an arm around her and kissed her forehead. "Ready?" he said.

She squinted and smiled in the soft elevator lights, "Yes, but I think this voyage is going to be a real doozy."

Avior chuckled, "Yeah, it will be. But with everyone together, we'll be fine."

Zovi nodded.

Kai's truck was already in the parking lot of Avior's condo building. Avior heard a whistle and saw Kai waving them over from across the beach, where the entire team was assembled. The team had carried two outrigger canoes over and laid them on the sand. Both canoes had four seats, and each canoe was tightly streamlined so that it would cut the water like a knife.

"All right, listen up," Kai said authoritatively. "As I already told you all, this is our final trial before Avior aligns with the Interverse. This outrigger canoe voyage from Oahu to Maui should take about twelve hours. I will take rear with Avior, Zovi, and Yelangelo in canoe one. Dallas, you take rear in canoe two with Midas, Cove, and Kangaroo." Kangaroo looked happy that he was part of the team and had a cool new nickname. Midas smiled at him and clapped him on the back.

"I have my equipment with me to keep us on track, as does Dallas for canoe two," Kai continued. "It really boils down to our food, water, sunscreen, determination, and teamwork." Kai had his hands proudly placed on his hips as he stared at the team. "Everybody, hands in. Triumph, on three!" Everybody circled up and put their hands in the middle. "One, two, three!" Kai shouted.

"Triumph!" Avior, Zovi, Midas, Cove, Dallas, Yelangelo, and Kangaroo all yelled together happily. With that yelp of glee, the team grabbed their respective outrigger canoes and stoically marched straight into the ocean, just as the sunrise crested the horizon.

With the outrigger canoe in the water, Avior jumped in the lead seat and looked around. Zovi was lithely lifting herself into the seat behind him, and Yelangelo was muscling into the seat behind her. Kai made sure the canoe was all situated then sprang into his rear seat. Avior turned his head and chuckled as he saw Midas's trademark tongue-out face in the lead seat of canoe two. Cove was paddling hard directly behind him with Kangaroo behind her and Dallas bringing up the rear.

"Everybody, paddle hard! We must get out over these shore waves!" Kai bellowed over the water. The whole team was paddling fiercely, fighting to stay straight as they began plowing through the oncoming waves. "If we turn sideways, these waves are going to flip us!" Kai shouted out. "Paddle! Paddle! Paddle!" Avior was putting his whole back into each paddle, but their work was paying off. Both canoes rose over one last wave just before it broke on top of them. With relief spread across their faces, the team steered into the clear beyond the waves breaking by the shore.

"Well done, everyone! Well done," Kai said solidly. Zovi tapped Avior on the shoulder, and he turned around. "Better get a good look. We won't be near land for a while," she said.

Avior nodded and let his eyes absorb the sunrise scene of the Waikiki beach. Then, with a smile, his eyes drifted back to Zovi's eyes. He winked. "I'm actually looking forward to being out in open water." Zovi's eyes opened wide. "I've never been out on the open ocean before," Avior continued. "I'm looking forward to being able to look around with absolute clarity at the water."

"Hmm, yeah, that does sound pretty cool," she said, as she muscled a couple of paddles. "The open ocean can be scary though. All alone, on the expanse, with the horizon on all sides…"

"Fortunately," Kai interrupted, "we should be able to see Maui for most of the voyage. That will keep our bearings straight."

The whole team sank into a rolling rhythm, paddling away from Oahu toward Maui. Every now and then, Avior would grin as he heard Midas from across the water telling stories and singing songs. Behind him Yelangelo would occasionally hum an African hymn that sounded warm and sunny. Kai kept the team on track, shouting out directions or advice as he monitored them closely. Cove had her hair down and was letting it blow in the sea breeze. Kangaroo seemed to be enjoying listening to Midas, his eyes darting happily over everything in sight. Dallas was the powerhouse of canoe two and kept them perfectly in line. Avior smiled. The front of his canoe was slicing the water like a knife, and he could see myriads of fish swimming beneath him. Zovi's loving voice would drift into his ear from time to time, and, as if in a dream, he would reply, happy as a clam.

The voyage was a serene one. It was about at the halfway mark that Kai pointed out a fast-moving storm cloud bank coming quickly toward them. He whipped out a satellite phone and punched one of the buttons. "Oh man, bad news, team!" he yelled loud enough for the other canoe to hear. "Those clouds aren't on the weather forecast. It's a squall. Probably spontaneous conditions churned it into being." The team all had their eyes fixed on the stormy clouds as they continued paddling. "I think we're going to have that bad bit hit us soon," Kai said gravely.

Kai was right. In almost no time at all, the squall was upon them. Dark skies, high winds, stinging rain, and waves whipped the sea up into whitecaps. Avior glanced around at the team. Everybody looked scared as they paddled hard, fighting to keep the canoes upright amid the random barrages of breakers. "Oh my god," Zovi said, right in Avior's ear. "This doesn't look good at all, Avior. This is exactly what was in the back of my mind when I was talking to you at the start of this voyage." Avior kept his steely gaze straight forward as a bolt of lightning crackled off to their side.

"Stay focused, everybody!" Kai bellowed over the squall. "This is a fight for our lives. *Do not* let your canoe tip over!" Avior was gripping his paddle like a vice as he stroked through the stormy seas. Suddenly their worst fear was realized. A rogue wave coming at an off angle pulled them up, up, up, and then with a sickening lurch in their stomachs, Avior, Zovi, Yelangelo, and Kai were pulled over the falls of the wave and turned upside down in the middle of the stormy ocean.

Avior was submerged for only a moment. But at that moment, the terror of the situation gripped his heart. He snarled and fought through his fear, swimming to the surface vigorously. "Zovi!" He called as he breached the surface.

"Avior!" came Zovi's voice about ten feet away through the misty rain-filled air.

"Stay calm, guys. Just take it easy," Kai said reassuringly from beside Zovi. Kai's calm voice soothed Avior.

Yelangelo surfaced right beside Avior, and he looked around wildly. "We must flip the canoe immediately!" he shouted as he choked on seawater.

"Yes, Yelangelo, Avior, Zovi, climb on top of the hull! When I push upward on the outrigger, you all grab hold of the canoe and rotate it around!" Kai said loudly but calmly. Avior made eye contact with Zovi and Yelangelo; then they all mounted the overturned hull and got handholds. "One, two, three!" Kai shouted. Kai pushed upward on the outrigger while

Avior, Zovi, and Yelangelo flipped themselves barrel roll style over with tight grips on the hull.

They were successful. The outrigger canoe flipped back over, and they all clambered back into their seats. "Where are the others?" Avior called, looking around for a sign of the other canoe.

Zovi choked back a sob of emotion, then got a grip on herself. "They've got to be right out of sight in this rain! We were only flipped for a few minutes!"

"Don't worry, I coached Dallas on what to do in just such a situation," Kai said seriously. "He will maintain course. As must we."

Avior nodded and looked around at Zovi and Yelangelo. They nodded solemnly.

Avior began paddling through the torrential downpour of the squall. Despite the choppy waters, they made fair progress moving forward. After about a half hour of chop and almost nonexistent visibility, the squall gave a final vicious gust, then passed over them. "Ahoy!" came a hearty shout from a ways away. Avior snapped his neck around and saw that as the squall's rain sheets passed, the second canoe had just emerged into clear skies.

"Ahoy!" Avior shouted back, waving at Midas, Cove, Kangaroo, and Dallas, who all looked shaken but relieved to be in the clear.

"Regroup!" Kai shouted out at the other canoe. Once Dallas had steered his group's canoe over, Kai cleared his throat loudly. "Well done, everyone. We were in a far more dangerous situation than I let on, but everybody maintained a level head and stuck together. Squalls are freak occurrences. It was never my intention to subject you to something so perilous. But Avior has little time left, and he needs this gritty endurance test to prepare him for what he must do." Kai looked around at them all, making sure to lock eyes with each person in turn. "We're pushing forward. Let's hydrate, eat, and get right back to it," he said resolutely.

Avior swung his ocean-eyed gaze around at Zovi and saw that she was slowly recovering from the scare. "Let's grab a bite," Avior said, comforting her with his warm words.

"Yeah…yeah, that sounds good," she said.

Avior could tell she was replaying the terrifying events in her head. "Hey, we're okay," he said reassuringly. "Life is full of crazy stuff. But don't worry, I'm here for you. And so are six other people. I was terror-stricken for an instant, but then I thought of you and the team and my purpose, and my mind cleared."

Zovi breathed a deep sigh as she let Avior's words clear her mind of the terrifying events of the squall.

As the two canoes floated side by side during their snack break, the silence was broken here and there by Yelangelo as he gently sang his warm African hymns. His songs calmed the team and reignited the sunlight of their hearts. By the end of their snack break, Yelangelo's hymns had cleared their minds of the terror of the squall, and everyone was feeling relieved and ready to get back to paddling on the open seas toward Maui.

The second half of their journey was a trying one, as they were getting exhausted, but everyone was determined to persevere. As they drew nearer to Maui, Avior looked over his shoulder and called back to Kai. "I still don't know what it is I will be doing when it comes time for me to try and obtain the Omniscript."

Kai was silent for a long moment, then replied, "The doctors have instructed me on what the process will be. Tomorrow at sunrise, we will all take you deep into the jungle. Aina Haina Valley should have sufficient space for you." Kai paused for a moment, then continued, "Because you WILL need lots of space. The doctors have also instructed me that to phase into the Interverse, you must meditate deeply, find clarity, and then let loose and sustain a primal scream with everything you've got. Hold that scream, because the force of your voice will match the Interverse wavelength present in you and will align. All the particles that make you up will emerge into that intersecting universe."

Avior looked skyward thoughtfully, taking this information in. "Once you're in the Interverse, you have about an hour to exert all the forceful energy you have," Kai continued. "The piezoelectric polymer-like space of the Interverse will respond by becoming charged by your energy force. That charge, if powerful enough, is what can trigger the Omniscript DNA to generate inside you. And don't forget, the black hole beings can slow you down. You'll have to switch yourself off to combat them, but switching yourself off is counterproductive to your mission. I will tell you the truth. Whatever happens, you will be a wreck afterward. Zovi will supervise your recovery, which could be extensive. I know this hurts to hear, but you are our only chance of obtaining the Omniscript. It's all or nothing." Avior, Zovi, and Yelangelo paddled silently for a while, absorbing Kai's words.

Quietly, so only Avior could hear, Zovi whispered, "Avior, please don't get yourself killed. I can do a full recovery for you, but I don't want to do a funeral."

Avior continued paddling, staring straight ahead, then turned slightly and whispered back, "I have to do what I have to do, no matter what happens." He could feel Zovi accept the truth in his words without even seeing her.

That evening, right around sunset, both outrigger canoes slid safely from the ocean onto the sandy shores of Maui. Avior pulled his aching body out of the canoe and sprawled out happily on the sand. The entire team came over and crashed peacefully next to him. Kai trooped over and stood before them, looking proud. "Beautiful work today, everyone. You should be very chuffed to have accomplished this endeavor." Exhausted, everyone nodded and murmured from their spots on the sand. Once they had rested, the team pulled the canoes up onto the beach. "Here are your plane tickets," Kai said, handing each teammate a flight ticket. "We'll all catch the flight back to Oahu. Get a good night's sleep, and then it will be Avior's day." Kai looked solemnly at Avior. "Avior, we will all be there for you. As your coach, through thick and thin, I deem you ready for your challenge." He stared at Avior seriously, but his expression was relaxed. "I believe in you. We believe in you." The team nodded in agreement, patting Avior on his head and shoulders.

As they made their way to the airport, Zovi held Avior's hand and never let go.

CHAPTER 9

THE INTERVERSE

After a night of being cloistered in his room, pacing endlessly and thinking of every possible scenario, Avior was still uneasy. He jolted out of his half asleep state and sprang up out of his bed. Kai had told him what was going to happen, but Avior still had no clue what it was going to be like once he was aligned into the Interverse.

He had a small but filling breakfast with coffee as he looked out of the window at the ocean. He felt ready to take on his destiny; however, he couldn't help but hear the tiny voice in his head that wondered if this would be his last breakfast. His phone buzzed on the table, and Avior checked the message that popped up. "Outside. It's time," the text from Kai read. Avior stood up and walked to the window. "Triumph," he growled to himself as he stared at the distant horizon.

A minute later, he was outside. He was going to miss this morning routine of walking out to meet the team at Kai's truck in the parking lot. He smiled as he rounded the corner and saw everyone piled high in Kai's truck. Each face radiated a reassuring faith in Avior that brought his chest out a little. "Mornin', tiger!" Zovi called out with a cheeky wink. "Hundred percent, this is your day!" she finished as she hopped out and gave him a tight hug.

"Yeah, you!" Midas shouted enthusiastically.

"We believe in you, Avior," Cove said peacefully as she gazed respectfully at him.

"You'll like going beast mode," Dallas commented.

"Wish I could try for the Omniscript. Sounds legendary." Yelangelo swung back his dreads and let loose an earthy African prayer chant to the sky.

Kangaroo popped a little three-sixty out of the back of the truck and took Avior's hand, "You will have great honor brought to you today. That is unquestionable."

The drive to Aina Haina Valley was an energetic one. Everybody was gassing Avior up, but Avior couldn't help but feel his hands shaking as he drew nearer to the unknown.

A short while later, Kai pulled the truck to a stop at the end of the road that backed up to the massive valley. Aina Haina was a sprawling, lush, jungly valley surrounded by high ridges except on the side where the road led up from the coast. "All right. We're going to hike into the middle," Kai said. He looked at Avior, then said, "Once you're aligned to the Interverse, you'll probably see the world differently. The world may even physically be different. I'm not sure. But the more room to move you have and obstacles to exert force on, the better." Kai gestured to the team, and everybody shouldered their packs and marched into the jungle.

Kai led the way, with Avior directly behind him. As they passed gnarled banyan trees, stream beds with blue pools, moss-covered boulders, and occasional sunlit clearings, Kai kept a continuous flow of pep talk and pointers. "You need to be forcing yourself to exert your energy at all times," he said. "Even if you fall, knock ten push-ups out then spring back up. It boils down to the fact that to stimulate the biological processes needed to generate the Omniscript, you're literally going to need to use every muscle, at all times, for as long as humanly possible, until you physically drop from exhaustion. You should be absolutely drained of energy down to zero by the end of your alignment in the Interverse." Avior hiked along behind Kai, memorizing everything he said.

The team hiked over a knoll covered in trees, then saw a large fern-covered glade in front of them. There were small boulders scattered around, with the largest one resting in the center of the clearing. "Here," Kai said. The team put their packs off to the side; then Kai motioned for Avior. "The natural vibrations of the jungle here should be a good pure place to switch from earth's wavelength to the Interverse wavelength." The team gathered close to Avior, their eyes moving between Kai and Avior.

"Stand on this central boulder here," Kai said as he gestured to the boulder in the middle of the glade. Avior wordlessly strode over and mounted the central boulder, throwing his gaze skyward. "Take deep breaths, focus your mind, find your core, and then I want you to belt out your most primal scream. Hold that scream as long as you can. Your body contains the frequency code for both universe's wavelengths, and with enough brute force in your scream, just like when you were fighting and skating and you morphed in-between for a second, that force can align you from one wavelength to the other."

Avior breathed deeply. He cleared his mind of all thoughts. He rid himself of everything that was floating through his head and found the bright burning core of energy that was simmering inside him like the sun. He steadied himself on the boulder. His eyes were closed, but he heard Zovi whisper, "Avior Aviideus," with such high regard in her voice that he felt himself swell up and he knew his time was here and now.

Avior opened his eyes, threw his head back, and flexed every muscle in his body as his lungs expelled a savage Viking-like primal scream that seemed to come from a primordial source deep in the back of Avior's soul. As if channeled through the eons of life on earth, Avior's long savage scream wrought the airwaves of the glade, and the earthly vision in his eyes phased into an alien spectrum of unbelievable colors.

The entire team stood back, startled, as they gazed at Avior's statuesque body atop the boulder, which now had laserlike beams of otherworldly light jetting from it. Avior's voice gave out, but he had made it. His laser-light-emitting body stood still for a moment, looking around, fists clenched. Zovi looked into Avior's eyes, and her jaw dropped. She saw the phantasmagoria of a different universe shining with colors unimaginable. Kai looked astounded but managed to yell out, "Go!"

Avior didn't seem to hear the sounds from earth's frequency anymore, but he knew what he had to do. He sprang up and flung a front flip off the boulder and then took off running. The team darted frantically after him.

Inside Avior's mind, everything suddenly made sense. He could see every atomic particle as it bonded with other suitable particles, forming everything in space. He could see light moving and plants photosynthesizing. As he ran, he realized that his very thoughts were projecting tiny quantum quarks into the space in front of him, laying out every possible course of action in this dreamlike space made of particles. He grabbed a hypertechnicolor tree branch as he ran past and felt the atoms of his hand meshing with the atoms of the branch. Avior realized he was a shining light of conscious energy moving through an oceanic field of atomic dreams immediately manifesting into realities.

Avior ran like he had never run before. He charged through this hypertechnicolor Interverse, smashing through ultra-multicolor foliage. He glanced at his legs and could see cuts bleeding super-silver-colored blood that ran like liquid mercury down his shins. Avior ran to a tree and grappled his way up the trunk, forcing every muscle to work as he went. He jumped from one tree to the next, muscling his way from branch to branch. He swung down to the ground and saw the forest floor ripple like water when he landed. He realized that the Interverse was malleable. With a savage smirk, he realized he was in a dream. He dove headfirst toward the forest floor, and from his willpower, he forced the particles of the ground to behave like a body of water. He swam through the sea of particles that comprised the forest floor. It mattered not what anything was; his consciousness could force it to be anything he wanted.

The team was running behind Avior, and they were absolutely losing their minds at what Avior was doing. The sight of Avior swimming through space, both the matter of the ground and the nothingness of open air, shattered their lifetime concept of reality. "OH, MY STARS!" Yelangelo managed to get out as he flabbergastingly tried to take in the sight of Avior. Midas was holding his head with both hands as he ran, his mouth agape. Zovi was sobbing. She had never seen something so beautiful, so divine. The laser-light illuminations emanating from Avior were casting beams on them all as they ran.

Avior did a swooping vortex dive through a tree trunk, his body passing through the particle membrane of the tree's matter. He stuck his hands into a car-sized boulder, and from his mind, he forced the particles of the large rock to switch frequency to a lighter state of being. He lifted the boulder, which now weighed as much as a barbell, and chucked it down a hill easily.

"Avior! Be careful! You could kill us!" Zovi shouted.

"I don't think he can hear us!" Kai shouted. Even Kai had trepidation in his voice. Avior was unleashing himself beyond what anyone had thought possible.

Suddenly a black hole being shot through the jungle and made a straight line toward Avior. Avior saw it coming, but now that he was in the Interverse and he knew how this space operated, he knew it stood no chance against him. It approached him as fast as a rocket, but Avior was ready. He forced the creation of a black hole opposite, a white hole, out of thin air with his mind. He gestured with his hands and forced the space between the black hole being and his created white hole to gravitationally magnetize together. The white hole, a created extension of Avior, was emitting energy, and the black hole being was feeding from it. The two were linked in a loop, and Avior knew what to do.

He approached the two forces of nature that were stuck in midair, looping the energy of each other, and held his hand out, just at the precipice of their event horizon. Avior channeled the energy that their cycle was creating and harnessed it for himself. In a moment, he had disintegrated the two and had charged himself with more energy.

The team was beyond dumbfounded at this point. Never in a million years had they ever dreamed of any of these events and possibilities. Kangaroo had a ghostlike look on his face, and with a glance, Zovi saw that he had lost his concept of reality. She ran over and slapped him, putting her face close to his. "Stay with it, Roo! Come on now!" She yelled. Cove grabbed Kangaroo's arm and dragged him along with her as Avior flew off through the canopy of the jungle.

"Stay with him!" Kai shouted.

Avior liked his newly discovered ability to fly. It was extremely taxing on his body and required enormous amounts of energy to sustain. It was the perfect way to combine all his training into exerting energy into the Interverse. He soared up a mountain spine that was heading toward the back of the valley. The space around him was glowing brighter and brighter as he flew. He looked at the information encoded in the atoms around him and saw that he was charging the piezoelectric space just as predicted. Space waved and glimmered around him like sheets of crystals. He saw a grassy bald at the summit of the ridge and swooped from his flight to land aggressively in the center of it. He was tired; flying had been as difficult as all his training challenges combined. But he knew he needed to zero out. He needed to exert every bit of force and energy he had.

In a moment of inspiration, Avior whipped his body into a tai chi stance. He had never trained in tai chi, but his body was extremely honed, and the movements seemed intuitive and natural to him.

He looked skyward as he flowed from position to position, his feet switching stances as he moved. He wrenched his hands upward and pushed the particles of the clouds with his mind. He could see now what his unleashed self looked like. Massive quantum streams of particles were blasting from him into the sky. He moved the clouds aside and brought forth the light of the sun, which to his Interverse eyes looked like strings of liquid diamonds oscillating onto the grassy bald of the summit.

In this new illumination on the summit of Aina Haina, Avior realized what he needed to do. He stood stock-still and placed his hands together in prayer. He churned up every ounce of energy he had left and focused his mind. He knew it was him, his mind, that had to obtain the Omniscript, not necessarily charged piezoelectric space. He imagined beams of pure particles projected from his mind and moved them through his body. He mentally elixered the Interverse particle constituents throughout every cell of his body, forcing the biological processes to work. The intricate work was demanding, but he made himself cultivate each atom in his body with his willpower, crafting not just one, but the entire genetic structure of the Omniscript sequence.

Avior stood, fully flexed, forcing every particle of his body to become the Omniscript for what seemed like an eternity. He was nearly complete, but he was on the verge of collapse. Just then, out of the brush, the team emerged, staring spellbound at Avior in his prayer state. Avior's knees were about to buckle and give out as he stood with his hands together, still forcing his body to create the Omniscript. Kai, Zovi, Midas, Cove, Dallas, Yelangelo, and Kangaroo walked over and crowded around Avior. They put their hands on him, supported him, held him up, and looked lovingly at him in his Interversal state.

Avior, who had had his eyes closed, opened them. He saw beings in front of him, comprised of vibrating strings of beautiful particles spinning around on their axes. It was divine to behold. As beings of particles, it was impossible to tell who was who, until one of the shorter beings moved in front of him. The being leaned in and planted a long loving kiss on his lips. Zovi. Avior smiled and felt his body subtlety click into place; then his eyes blinked slowly, and when they opened back up, he was staring at Zovi's gorgeous face. Avior smiled. He was back. His body gave out as he zeroed out, and the team gently caught his collapsing body and lowered him onto the earthen fragrance of the brilliant green grass.

CHAPTER 10

THE OMNISCRIPT

"Beautiful, absolutely beautiful," Avior heard a doctor say as he slowly emerged from a deep sleep. Avior's eyelids were heavy, and they took time to open. "I think he's coming to," Avior heard Zovi say in a hushed tone. Spurred by Zovi's voice, Avior fought to regain full consciousness. "Oh my god, what…did I…" Avior sputtered. The doctor put a gentle hand on Avior's shoulder. Avior's eyes focused, and he saw that the doctor was holding a small clear vial in front of him.

"This vial right here," the doctor said proudly, "has enough Omniscript to alter humankind forever." Avior's whole team was standing proudly in the room, with looks of golden affirmation shining on their faces. "We can synthesize this Omniscript endlessly," the doctor continued, "and with this, we can obliterate earthly diseases and help people maintain youthful bodies and minds for as long as two lifetimes, if they want to, of course." The doctor clasped his hands and sighed with relief. "We also should be able to create the much-anticipated push toward the next phase of human evolution. Our planet needs us to step up and become the vision we see for the future. And you, Avior Aviideus, have granted us the key to that very destiny." The doctor smiled. "That is why we have decided to name this next step in human evolution after you. The next stage of humanity shall be called *Homo Deus*, after your last name, Aviideus."

The doctor straightened up and happily started clapping his hands. Kai, Zovi, Midas, Cove, Dallas, Yelangelo, and Kangaroo warmly applauded Avior. "You did it, my man, you did it," Midas said excitedly. Cove leaned in and kissed Avior on the cheek. Dallas grabbed Avior's hand; then Yelangelo and Kangaroo crowded in and patted his shoulders.

Avior looked up as his faithful coach Kai came over. "I am beyond proud of you, Avior. I put you up against my most difficult challenges, and through thick and thin, you persevered and came out the victor. You have proven many things to me. You have proven that you can operate at Olympic levels of physical ability. You have proven that even though you have a fully digital upbringing in the Simulation, you are capable of soulful love." Kai motioned to Zovi, who was by his side, smiling. "And you have proven the immense power of teamwork." Kai looked at the team. "I am honored to have been your coach, and I am honored that each of you joined this team, this mission, this vision." Midas, Cove, Dallas, Yelangelo, and Kangaroo nodded at Kai.

"Well, what's next?" Avior asked inquisitively.

The doctor stepped in. "There are talks of a Nobel Prize," the doctor said as he looked at Avior. "And governments across the world are already allocating money to this team for your work in obtaining the Omniscript." The doctor's eyebrows raised. "I know that we were all winging it with such a tight time frame, and there wasn't much talk of compensation, but it seems there may be more in store for you all as a reward than anybody ever dreamed of." Everybody's eyes were wide as the doctor's words hit them. The doctor smiled warmly with his gentle bedside manner. "The future is going to be very bright, very bright indeed."

Three years later, the world was a vastly different one. The Omniscript had been introduced to the population of the earth, and disease was now non-existent. The youth of the world, now called *Omnis*, would be able to stay youthful for double, if not triple, the length of time from previous generations. Abundance prevailed across the globe, and in some ways, real life seemed similar to the Simulation. Only the old-timers jokingly grumbled about things.

The team, collectively, was granted over one hundred billion dollars. They were invited to attend world-televised events and meet the likes of Elon Musk, Jeff Bezos, Mark Zuckerberg, Richard Branson, and other world changers.

Kai built a chain of successful gyms across America called *Force Source*. He regularly travels, teaching classes, and is always booked to help train Olympic athletes.

Midas bought a mansion in Los Angeles and got into acting. He specializes in action comedy and insists on doing his own stunts. He instantly became a Hollywood household name with his goofy, kid-next-door swagger, and comical charm. Always up for fun, he loves driving his Lamborghinis and Ferraris around the country in secret Cannonball Run races.

Cove moved to Fiji and now owns one of the famous overwater bungalow resorts. She spends her time surfing, hiking, making music, and taking romantic beach walks with her handsome Fijian boyfriend. Some of her songs took off on American radio, and she stays active recording from her studio in her private bungalow.

Dallas went on to fight in the UFC, claiming two featherweight division victories. Dallas partnered up with Kai and his Force Source gyms and stays active teaching mixed martial arts classes across the country. Always seen with a different famous actress or model, Dallas stays in the media's limelight, always rocking a stoic expression.

Yelangelo continues to pour forth his considerable wealth into his home country of Africa. He has become quite a philanthropist and has created many charities and platforms to promote and encourage healthy development in countless African communities. He built a lavish compound outside the little village he grew up in and has taken up being "the man-about-town." He continues to train as a bicyclist and loves coming across children in the street and handing out hundred-dollar bills.

Kangaroo finished his schooling and went on to become an architect. With every building he designs, he always incorporates a plethora of skateable obstacles and surfaces as part of the project. His vision is very Zen-oriented, with gentle swooping lines crafting his buildings and plazas into futuristic places where work and play flow seamlessly together.

And as for Avior and Zovi, the Omniscript was only the beginning of happily ever after. They traveled the world, soaking in all the sights, tasting all the local cuisines, and learning from all cultures. After their travels, they bought a comfortable house together on Oahu, and on one windy summer day, Avior stood beside Zovi on the balcony of the house, looking down off the mountain at the coastline of Honolulu.

"You know, I've been thinking," Avior said with a smile as he looked out at the beauty of the Hawaiian island.

"Whatcha been thinking about?" Zovi asked, turning her head to look at Avior.

Avior slowly turned his head to look at Zovi, then knelt on one knee and pulled a diamond ring from his pocket that sparkled like the North Star. "About everything we've been through. Meeting at China Walls that one day, then going through all those crazy challenges, then fighting to obtain the Omniscript, and then traveling the world; I feel like we've packed a lifetime of life into a short span of living. And through it all, you've been there for me, and I've been there for you. Each of us is so disciplined in our own regard, and I feel if we solidify that discipline into the discipline of us, we can make something like never before." Zovi's jaw was gently agape, and a shining tear was in her eye.

"The Omniscript to me is that bond we created when we were striving to obtain the key to the future of humanity. And just as we were striving to obtain that key for all humanity, I want to strive to obtain that key for your future. I want to see what heights we can attain. With each word, with each look, with each move, raising the level of each moment. Just like how the DNA sequence of the Omniscript works by combining the best possible combinations of its base pairs, I want to form a sequence like that with you. I want to see what THAT can become. Zovi Zelleven, will you marry me?"

Zovi had the most definite look on her face as she pulled Avior to his feet and brought his head toward hers. Her soft lips met his, and they moved across each other, the taste of strawberry lip balm bringing a smile to Avior's lips. "A hundred percent, yes," Zovi whispered straight to Avior's face, lifting her eyes from Avior's lips to his eyes.

Together, Avior and Zovi did just what Avior had told her he wanted to do. They lived each moment like the Omniscript, sharing helping words, reinforcing each other through their days with knowing looks, and moving gracefully through their lives. And all the while, they maintained their training regimen. On occasion, they would share a look over an exercise, and the eighteen-year-old kid in each of them would shine through, smiling at the beauty of it all.

With the help of the International Board of Education, Avior started a school for children that was constructed in orbit around earth called *the Sequence*. The school combined artificial gravity environments, zero gravity environments, and environments augmented with the Simulation to create a premier educational space that doubled as a platform for elite-level athletes.

Avior stood with his arms folded behind him and stared out of the window at the blue-green jewel of Earth in front of him. He was a chiseled twenty-five-year-old man now, and one of the teachers at the Sequence. He heard the door to his chamber open, and he looked around. Zovi, dressed in her athletics director uniform, was striding up to him. "King of the world, yeah?" she said jokingly.

"We all are," Avior said quietly.

Zovi smiled and turned to look out of the window at earth. "You know," she said slyly, "seeing all these children in this incredible school, combining their education with their physical training, gets me thinking."

Avior raised his eyebrows at the sly tone in her voice. "Yeah? What's going through your mind?" he asked.

Zovi chuckled, then said, "We need an Avior 2.0. Whether it's a boy or a girl, earth needs another superstar."

Avior motioned to the school around him, "Well, there's plenty of children here that can rise to the occasion. I saw that young Mattias Matthews really stepping up recently, and his sister has really got some powerful legs on her…" Avior trailed off as he saw the look in Zovi's eyes.

"What about our own little superstar?" Zovi whispered. Avior's eyebrows really raised this time. Then he looked confidently out at earth through the window.

"A baby, you say?" He turned back to look at Zovi; then they both broke out laughing. "Oh, my stars! This baby is going to be born into the most beautiful time earth has ever seen!" Avior said enthusiastically. He straightened up, clasped his hands, and hummed a little melody to himself, then winked at Zovi. "I'd love to have a little superstar running around the Sequence. Hundred percent."

Jonathan Wade Barrow has a bachelor of science in communications from the University of Tennessee, Knoxville. Jonathan loves tropical islands and has lived on Saint John in the US Virgin Islands, as well as Maui and Oahu in the Hawaiian Islands. His favorite pastimes are skateboarding and cliff diving.

www.ingramcontent.com/pod-product-compliance
Lightning Source LLC
Chambersburg PA
CBHW022020150726
47990CB00002B/746